G

The Ghastling

XVII

IN THIS ISSUE

THE GHASTLING No. 17

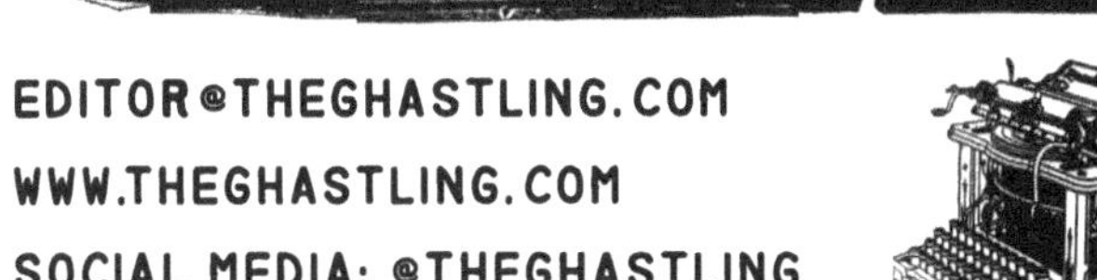

The Fetch would like to thank Patreon supporter Aaron Spink for sponsoring this omen and keeping impending death alive...

EDITOR
Rebecca Parfitt

GRAPHIC DESIGNER
Wallace McBride

EDITORIAL ASSISTANT
Tracey Rees

SPECIAL THANKS
J&C Parfitt & Andrew Robinson

CONTACT THE GHASTLING

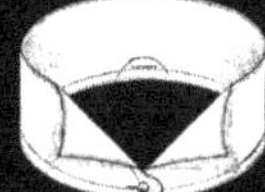

EDITOR@THEGHASTLING.COM

WWW.THEGHASTLING.COM

SOCIAL MEDIA: @THEGHASTLING

ISSN: 2514-815X
ISBN: 978-1-8381891-6-7

PUBLISHED BY THE GHASTLING

Copyright remains with the individual authors and artists. No part of this magazine may be reproduced, except for the purposes of review, without the prior permission of the publisher.

The Ghastling gratefully acknowledges the financial support of the Books Council of Wales.

The Ghastling

Tales of Ghosts, the Macabre and the Oh-So Strange

THE HEADLESS HORSEMAN

Wyn Lewis

Martha

Pamela Koehne-Drube

Victoria Day

OUR PATRONS ARE OUR LIFE'S BLOOD

LEND US YOUR FEAR ... JOIN THE GHASTLING ON PATREON!

$1

THE ECTOPLASM
You receive our eternal thanks and access to patron only feed.

$2

THE SEANCE
For those who wish to summon the words: a monthly writing prompt straight into your inbox.

$3

THE POLTERGEIST
Your name listed on our supporter page on the website, a monthly writing prompt and access to patron only feed.

TO JOIN THE PATRONS OF THIS CLUB VISIT PATREON.COM/THEGHASTLING

EDITORIAL

REBECCA PARFITT

Dear Reader,

Welcome to the haunted and peculiar world of Book 17. This issue is guaranteed to slip you a bit of the weird, the uncomfortable, the creepy, topped up with a garnish of terror. I think it's what we all need right now - a little distraction, a little something fun to raise the heart-rate and set our imaginations alight. The stories within will twist your perspective and leave you with a funny feeling in your gut. That's fear for you.

In Warren Benedetto's 'Uncle Pumpkin's Tongue', a seemingly innocent fairground ride turns into something revoltingly sinister - you wouldn't want your kids having a go on that ride... but the fairground: is it ever really a safe place for children? In Paul Buchanan's thoroughly disturbing tale, 'The Bynum Girl', a community anticipates the release of one of its most terrifying members: a girl who once tormented them all. They

prepare for the worst, wondering, will she ever really be safe enough to be let out...? JP Relph's mind bending story, 'Delirus', tells of a doll, kept out of sight in the basement of a house gathering dust. She is discovered by a little girl who becomes quite taken with her. But what the little dolly harbours inside will make your skin crawl... Reggie Chamberlain-King's, 'Living With It', is a deeply troubling story of a mother unravelling in her domestic surroundings. Has she really just committed the most unmotherly act? Where is her son, really? Rory Say's thought provoking story, 'The Other Door', tells of a boy who keeps finding a door in strange places, but one that he cannot ever open. In Mark Blayney's, eerie story, 'Coin, Mirror, Manoeuvre', a man lives alone in the woods surrounded by his memories of an unrecognisable past - familiar, yet, unfamiliar. Something utterly life-changing has happened, but what? And which version of events is correct...? 'The Catafalque' by

Victoria Dowd is a spine-chilling story of a couple who convert a disused chapel, novel indeed, but is it ever a good idea to use a catafalque as a dining table? In Eve Chancellor's story inspired by true events, 'The Resurrection Man', a corpse-hauler delivering freshly dead bodies receives a visit from someone unexpected prompting a series of disturbing events. It is 1916 in Neil A. Wilson's, 'In the Bleak Midwinter', and an invalid soldier is convalescing in Marsham Hall after a mustard gas attack. He should be improving but the nightmares keep leaking in, getting worse, almost as though something is tormenting him on purpose...

I do hope you enjoy these nine brilliant stories from both new and seasoned Ghastling authors. And thanks to each and every one of you for purchasing a copy of this magazine - we appreciate you to the grave and back!

Sleep tight, I hope the nightmares don't keep you up at night...

Rebecca Parfitt
Editor
The Ghastling

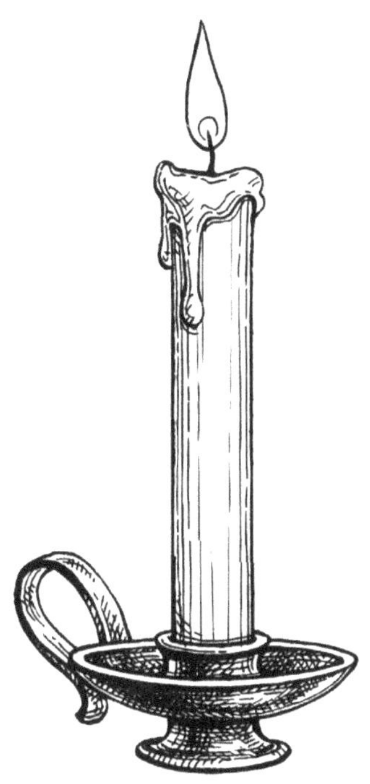

Uncle Pumpkin's Tongue

by Warren Benedetto

Illustrated by Andrew Robinson

I wish I had warned someone about Uncle Pumpkin. Maybe I could have stopped him. Maybe I could have saved those poor kids.

But until recently, I had no memory of the man at all. It was only after the bodies of the missing children were found—one boy still clutching a deflated pumpkin balloon in his shriveled, blackened hand—that I remembered what happened that night. And I realized that one of those kids could have been me.

Every October, the Rafferty Family Farm hosted a spectacular autumn carnival known as Uncle Pumpkin's Festival of Fun. The festival's centerpiece was the giant slide towering over the fairgrounds. Officially, it was called the Great Slide, but all the kids called it by its unofficial moniker: Uncle Pumpkin's Tongue. It was an apt nickname. The top of the ride was framed by an enormous plywood facade hand-painted to resemble the face of the festival's mascot, Uncle Pumpkin: flat black irises, thick eyebrows, and a twisting mustache over a gaping, open-mouthed smile. A red plastic slide protruded from the center of the mouth like a tongue, descending through a series of stomach-dropping humps and ending in a long straightway with hay bales stacked at the end.

Hour after hour, kids climbed the wooden staircase to the top of the slide, where a seasonal employee—usually a teen from the local high school—handed each of them a frayed burlap sack to sit on. The kids lined up five across, one in each lane of the slide, waiting for a shout of "Ready? Set? Go!" from one of the attendants. Then the riders pushed off and zipped down the slide on the sacks, each secretly hoping to be going fast enough to crash into the hay bales stacked at the end of the straightway.

My parents encouraged me to try the Great Slide every year, but I always refused. It wasn't the slide that scared me, it was the character of Uncle Pumpkin that I found most terrifying. He was supposed to be a silly, clown-like figure that brought joy to children around Halloween, but the only thing he brought to me was a sense of profound unease, a lingering dread that left me feeling like I had a sandbag in my stomach.

The face painted above the slide was scary enough, but the actual Uncle Pumpkin—the one roaming the festival grounds with a bouquet of pump-

kin-shaped balloons—was even worse. His real name was Joe Rafferty, the middle-aged grandson of the original Uncle Pumpkin, his Grandpa Fred. Joe wore the same oversized black suit, orange bow tie, and crushed fedora that his grandfather wore in the 1940s. The classic Uncle Pumpkin features were smeared thick and messy across his pale, pockmarked face, as if he had applied the grease paint with the chewed end of an old hot dog. His mouth reeked of cigarettes and spoiled chicken, with yellowed teeth that leaned and twisted like they were trying to escape from his receding gums. He enjoyed sneaking up behind kids and poking them in the side with a bellowing "Boo!" before handing them a balloon to quell their startled tears. The schtick was intended to be funny, but it always felt cruel to me.

As I grew older, my refusal to go down the Great Slide became a liability, especially when my friends rode it without a second thought. Finally, when I was ten, my friend Simon convinced me to give it a try.

After saying goodbye to my parents—possibly for the last time, I feared—I began the tortuous ascent up the rickety stairs toward the top of the slide. The line seemed to take forever. The higher we went, the colder the steady autumn wind got. By the time it was my turn to ride, my teeth were chattering, and my fingers were numb.

"Lane Five." The attendant handed me a burlap sack to sit on, then pointed to the far end of the platform. I froze, too petrified to go any further. I tried to will my legs to move, but they wouldn't respond. I was paralyzed with fear.

After waiting a few seconds, Simon nudged me in the back. "Go!"

"I'm going!" I took a hesitant step, trying not to look down at the ant-sized people on the fairgrounds far below. I imagined my parents smiling proudly up at me from the bottom of the slide, having no idea that their beloved son was about to soil his jeans.

Simon put his hands on my shoulders and guided me forward. "Come on. Let's move." He positioned me in front of Lane Five, took his seat in Lane Four, then patted the red plastic in my lane. "Here. Sit."

I flapped the burlap out flat on the slide, carefully settling my backside down onto it and closing my eyes. In the distance, I could hear squeals of glee from the carnival rides mixing with the twang of country western music from the stage in the barn. A strong gust of wind pushed against my back, carrying with it the smell of cigarettes and rotten chicken. Suddenly, I was overwhelmed by a powerful wave of vertigo that threatened to topple me forward down the slide. I grabbed for the sides of my lane to steady myself. But instead of cold plastic, my hands touched something else. Something warm. Something wet.

Gasping with revulsion, I yanked my hands away. My eyes snapped open. The blood drained from my face.

The fairgrounds were gone, replaced by a featureless void that merged with the starless sky above. Simon was gone, too, as were all my other friends, the attendants, and everyone else waiting in line. The sound of the festival had been replaced with a silence so absolute that my brain could only process it as a sort of rushing hiss. I was utterly alone at the top of the slide. Except, it wasn't a slide anymore. It was a tongue. A real tongue.

Uncle Pumpkin's Tongue.

The slide had transformed from shiny red plastic into dull pink flesh, rippling with papillae and slicked with saliva.

The tongue snaked out into the darkness beneath me, so impossibly long that it seemed to disappear over the horizon. The warmth of its flesh radiated through the burlap as the saliva soaked into my jeans and dampened the backs of my thighs. A drop of hot liquid splattered onto my forehead from above and ran down over my eye. I swiped it away with the back of my wrist, then looked up. Overhead, rotting yellow teeth protruded from gums blackened with disease. Elongated drips of drool dangled from cracked and bleeding lips.

I was in Uncle Pumpkin's mouth. And if I didn't get out of there right away, I knew he would swallow me whole. I'd slide down his throat and into a churning acid bath filled with half-digested chunks of kids just like me, dissolving in a vile stew of melted flesh and bubbling fat.

With a desperate cry, I closed my eyes and threw my weight forward, away from Uncle Pumpkin's rotten maw. I felt myself falling, picking up speed as I slid down the spit-slicked tongue. I opened my mouth to scream, but all that came out was a strangled moan of terror. Stinking droplets of foul spittle splattered against my face and neck as I accelerated, plummeting faster and faster through a series of nauseating drops, then rocketing off the end of the tongue and into the infinite nothingness beyond…

…where I slammed feet-first into a bale of hay. Cheers erupted. I opened my eyes to see a crowd of festival-goers applauding me. The noise of the festival returned, warbling unsteadily like a record player picking up speed.

Simon crawled over to me, an expectant look on his face. "Well? What'd you think?"

"Fun," I mumbled, still confused and disoriented by what just happened. "It was fun."

I turned and looked back up the slide. It was just as it had always been: a painted Uncle Pumpkin face at the top, with a red plastic slide descending to the ground. Whatever I experienced up there must have been my imagination, an insane hallucination brought on by panic and fear.

Relieved that the nightmare was over, I climbed to my feet, returned the burlap sack to the pile by the stairs, and followed Simon through the ride's exit. As we merged into the crowd, a sharp finger jabbed into my side. I yelped and spun around. Uncle Pumpkin was behind me, leering at me with a nicotine-stained grin. My bladder loosened, threatening to dump a flood of urine down my pants. I felt an overwhelming urge to run, but my legs had turned into useless sacks of grain. There was nothing I could do but stand there in fearful silence.

Uncle Pumpkin motioned like he wanted to tell me a secret. Then he bent down, his face drawing within an inch of my ear. He cupped his hand around his mouth as if to prevent anyone from hearing what he was about to say ... then dragged his tongue along the length of my ear in a long, wet stroke. The stink of cigarettes and rotten chicken assailed my senses as he spoke in a breathy whisper.

"Boo."

Then he took my hand, pressed the string of a balloon into my palm, and ambled off into the crowd without another word.

I wiped at my ear with my sleeve, desperate to remove the film of foul-smelling spit the man's tongue had left on my skin. Tears welled in my eyes.

"What did he say?" Simon asked.

I should have told him what happened, but I didn't. I couldn't. Instead, I said, "Nothing." I shrugged. "Just Happy Halloween."

Then I opened my palm and let go of the balloon, watching as it spiraled skyward into the cold October night.

The Ghastling

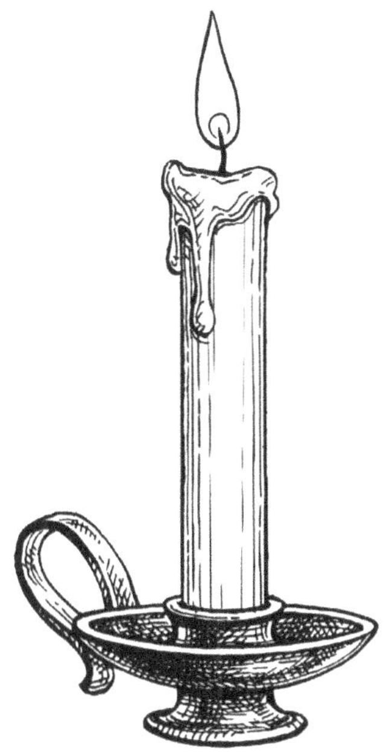

The Bynum Girl

by Paul Buchanan

That October rumours blew through Wulf Landing like wind off the lake. No one had spoken of the Bynum girl in a decade.

Sure, we made glancing references, but no one uttered her name. Wulf Landing had fallen off the map, as far as the out-of-towners were concerned. We'd vanished from the pages of every village news-rag but our own. And—ask anyone—we preferred it that way. We were happy to sink into oblivion and turn our at- tention to the mundane, the benign, the harmless. We filled the bleach- ers at the high school games again, quarreled about Fords and Chevys, swapped Mason jars of what grew in our side yards.

We remembered the Bynum girl, of course, though the young- er among us—kids up at the high school, say—had only dim recollections of credenzas barricading doors, hundred-watt bulbs burning through the night, and siblings crowded in their parents' bedrooms. The young could not fathom their parents' strain that summer: ears pricked for footfalls on sun-scorched lawns, eyes probing the shadows through slots in the blinds, lips shaping silent profanities and prayers. Since the girl was a minor, most of the particulars were kept out of the papers, so, even if some curious kid did some digging, there was little to unearth.

After that summer, when they finally carted the girl away, our heady vigilance gradually waned—like the slow exhale of a long-held breath. Still, that October no one came trick-or-treating. We bought Butterfingers and Abba-Zabas at the Rexall but ate them all ourselves. When the first snow fell, it took a week or two not to flinch at our own children's small footprints arcing across the yard. When spring arrived, and our victory gardens needed tending, we found our hoes and shovels in the house, propped near doorways as makeshift weapons. One crisp March morning we lugged them out the kitchen door, feeling sheepish, and stowed them back in the garden shed. By the Fourth we left windows wide to court the breeze and fanned ourselves on porches, dreading only horseflies.

☠

All that was years ago, but now speculation and scuttlebutt gusted through the streets again like dogwood leaves.

First, Reggie Layton from the Post Office let slip that the girl's mother had got two registered letters from the institution. Both arrived the same Tuesday. On one the address was typed; on the other it was written in a fine womanly script that, to Reggie, looked faintly European. (The numeral seven, he would later recollect, was crossed like a lower-case *t*.) Both envelopes were thick number-10s, and each had the institution's name embossed in the top left corner. Reggie had walked up the front path and pushed them through the mail slot. They landed on the hall floor with a *thunk* he could hear from out on the porch. So, the rumor went around that maybe she would be released. We shook our heads: unlikely, after all that happened.

But then her mother—God bless her—was down at the Kreskies buying clothes that were too small to be for her—dungarees and tees; a pair of Converse shoes; a pullover sweater; and a six-pack of white cotton panties, size x-small. The same day, at the Woolworth, she bought new twin-sized sheets and a bedspread, using a coupon clipped from the *Shopper*. Tennie Larrison slipped the purchases into a twine-handled shopping bag and asked if they were expecting visitors. The old woman pursed her lips and kept her silence. She scurried back out to the street, head ducked low.

Bob Vanderford was of the opinion that the girl could not be cured and that it would never be safe to let her out, but he'd read somewhere that a change in federal law meant the girl could not be held against her wishes—she was, after all, no longer a minor. This did not sound right to us, given what the girl had done, but Bob owns the big hardware store on Greenleaf. His mind is tough as nails, sharp as lever shears. His opinions are rivet strong. He's not a man we question.

☠

And so, the talk started up again. We rummaged up old stories, unfolded them, and smoothed them flat on any table we gathered around.

Dana Foulk, down at Quincy's Market, spoke of how, feeling sorry for the Bynum girl, she'd years ago dragged her twin nieces to a backyard birthday. Naturally, the Bynum girl was schooled at home, but the entire second-grade class at Horace Mann got invitations. The late Mrs Porterfield, teacher at that time, had plodded up and down the rows dutifully passing out the envelopes. She shot each student a stern look as she pressed the invitation on their desktops. Before dismissing the class that afternoon, she plucked the trash bin from beside her desk and set it by the doorway. Most of the children understood what they were to do.

Still, Dana Foulk, feeling it her Christian calling, took the twins. There was a magician, she later reported, a rented canopy, and a fancy sheet cake from Stowe's. Few kids showed up—none without a guardian. It was a late April Saturday (before that fateful summer) and the long shadows of afternoon still held a chill. Despite the cold, guests were penned in the back garden, between the porch and the tree line. No one was invited inside. Dana and the twins lingered a polite hour, let the magician reach his steel-ring finale, then conjured an excuse to leave. The gift bags they brought home held not just candy and whistles, but real Timex watches, transistor radios, and silver dollars.

There were those in town who maintained that the Bynum girl had been mute. Others claimed to have heard her singing from the upstairs dormer window—a voice high and tremulous, a tune no one could name. Whether she had a voice or not, we all knew she could see. She watched us. For a season, Frank and Laurel Leach rented the house across the street. They spoke of seeing the girl behind the garden hedge at dawn, piling leaves or weaving daisy chains. They'd see her gazing blankly from a front porch swing at hours no child should be awake.

When Bonnie Templeton walked her corgi down Gilroy Street, the Bynum girl would track their progress from the front bay window. Baxter would tuck his tail and slink towards the street, tugging at his leash. Eventually he'd stop before they even turned the corner, belly down, paws dug in. Bonnie had to find another route.

We dusted off every old offense and oddity. Poor Agnes Lockwood reduced to ashes in her own front room. That whole calendar year when every baby born was male. The patch of lakeside thimbleweed that bloomed one January, through two feet of snow. These were just a few of the incidents recalled in diner booths or on the row of scooped plastic seats at the Laundromat. The Sunday sermon at First Methodist—"Wherefore Do the Wicked Live?"—made no direct references to the Bynum girl, but its subtext was clear.

☠

It's true: we were afraid, though no one said as much. Bob Vanderford's store ran out of yard lights, and he had to put them on backorder. The same was true for surface bolts and security bars. Ed Night sold his entire shipment of Remington 870s the Saturday morning they arrived from Ilion, along with every box of cartridges on the shelves. (Geese, his buyers said; we all knew better.) Neighbors snatched up Marge Menaker's litter of Rottweiler pups the weekend they were weaned. The rest of us left porch lights burning day and night. We sawed down broomsticks to block our latch-less windows. We made a dusk ritual of checking locks and latches. We blamed the heat for our sleeplessness, or that after-dinner coffee, or the nightjar's call from the tree line.

The whole Dederer family (across

the street and two houses down) offered a flimsy excuse to head north and stay with family in Marquette. Randy got a leave of absence from the firehouse. They pulled the kids out of school (even though the youngest had already been held back a year). But who among us could blame them? We'd have done the same if we had well-off kin.

☠

When a few cats disappeared, followed by Mrs Webber's old, blind dachshund, no one bothered to call *The Herald's* classifieds or staple fliers to telephone poles. We knew the girl was back. We took such small losses in stride and braced for what was to come. A pet was one thing, we told ourselves, as we climbed the stairs to check again on our sleeping children.

Lois Shaynor was the first casualty. She'd skipped dinner one Tuesday night, feeling faint. Frank fixed himself a cold beef sandwich and joined her on the sofa for *The Rifleman*. A few minutes in, Lois bolted upright, howled and vomited pins and straw onto the *Better Homes and Gardens* fanned on the coffee table. She was still alive when Frank got her to the Greenwood hospital.

"Drinking straws?" the ER attendant asked, looking up wide-eyed from her clipboard.

"No," Frank told her. "Straw, like you'd put in a paddock or weave into baskets. And *pleating* pins, I think they're called."

Lois was already unconscious when they got her on the gurney. For three days, she tossed and turned and spoke gibberish. Her son drove up from Bone Springs, and her daughter flew in from Seattle. She died Friday morning, staring bulge-eyed at the ceiling. "Peritonitis and intra-abdominal hemorrhage," the death certificate read. What doctor would click

his Parker pen and jot word "bewitched"?

After she was put in the ground and the kids went home, Frank started drinking Old Grand-Dad most nights at Kelsey's Downtown Pub, where he occupied the last stool by the men's room door. The rest of us gave him elbow room. We ignored his muttering. We looked at him and then took our turns at the payphone to check in at home.

All through October we held our breaths—because, well, it was October. Pumpkins rotted at the grocery. No one went near the Rexall candy shelves. Halloween night we hunkered down. Our porch lights burned, but no doorbells rang. No sheet-clad kids ventured up our unraked paths. All Saints Day dawned quietly. Maybe that was a good omen. We allowed ourselves a little hope.

☠

Mike Sutter claimed he actually saw the girl on the Bynum's back steps the second week of November when he was raking up the Stapleton's leaves for spare change. He claimed that—somehow—the girl hadn't aged. She looked, he told us, just like in the decade-old Baptist church directory, the only photo of her we had.

None of us believed him, of course. Mike had been a shooting guard on the high school team, a big clean-cut kid who seemed destined for Ann Arbor or at least East Lansing. But the summer after graduation, he cut off three toes with a jackhammer, and after that he took to drink. For the last decade, he'd been quaffing 40s from a paper sack, sleeping in church basements, waiting out rainstorms in the park's gazebo. There was little reason to believe the man.

But then, a week before Thanksgiving, Mike was found behind the Chevron Station by the river in a stand of poplars. To find him dead—at long last—was no surprise. But then the rumor went around that his open eyes were shelled with hardened candle wax. The night he died, Becca Welsh found an arrangement of 13 polished pebbles on her WELCOME mat when she came home from choir practice. The morning he was found, strange birds circled high overhead.

For the next few days, all over town, we heard a strange, steady tone, a high note with a buzz to it. Indoors it seemed to be coming from the next room. Outside it was always behind you, over your right shoulder. We ransacked cupboards and trailed the sound through the streets, but it seemed to have no source. Miss Brenner, who taught music at the high school, found it on her piano: a G above high C. We went to bed with pillows pressed to our ears and when we woke the sound was gone, but the trees around the spot where Mike's body was found were stripped of their leaves, as if winter had come in a single night.

Ted Van Landers was the next to die— but again that was no surprise. He rode fast and never wore a helmet. He liked to steal up behind you and roar past when you least expected it, making your heart thud. They found the bike first, the only blue Indian in town. Some rowing-team boys had snuck a case of Fallstaff into the Klempner's barn, and there the motor- cycle was, leaning on its kickstand in the breezeway. They forgot the beer and tried to start the thing, but none knew how. Timmy Bowers, the coxswain, told his dad the next morning. Mr. Bowers called the police.

Volunteers searched the whole farm. We beat the bushes and combed the acre of woods at the back. By nightfall some- one found Ted in a tractor-oil drum that had already been searched. Head trauma, the autopsy said. Blunt force. They buried him down in La Porte, where his sister's husband owned a couple of dry-cleaning stores.

Kelsey's Downtown Pub became our rumor clearinghouse. We all gathered there to compare and compile—even Pastor Trip, even Margie Starling, whose father died of Bushmills. Each night we circled the scarred tables and filled the two Naugahyde booths, neighbors coming and leaving throughout the afternoon and night. We sat on the stools with our backs to the bar, listening to whoever was hold- ing forth. Ed Marr's rider mower wouldn't start; for decades it had been reliable as sunrise. Two of Vicki Salazar's cats—both the black ones—refused to eat. The Spell- man's new color TV kept switching off, though the remote was on the coffee table in plain sight.

Every once in a while, someone bought a pitcher of Olympia out of a sense of guilt—though Rick O'Brien, behind the bar, seemed not to care anymore if he made a dime. He stood, big and surly, in front of the ranks of amber bottles, arms folded, listening like the rest of us, his square brow creased in concentration.

And the stories kept coming through the pub's front door, a new tidbit with each arrival. Rosie Ward—who managed Gus Walker's construction company— found strange sounds on the company's answering machine each morning: dark, unintelligible muttering and the sound of wind. Aaron Georges had watched from an upstairs window while blue lights float- ed through his orchard, three feet off the ground. Ball lightning perhaps; perhaps something more sinister. The canned goods in Melody Lampkin's pantry—all unopened—turned up empty one morn- ing.

Countless small things went missing: figurines and vases from mantles, peel- ers and pie birds from kitchen drawers. Hub wrenches went AWOL from sedan trunks. Every last comb disappeared from the Hair Gallery one Monday morning.

Volume JEREZ–LIBE of the *Encyclopedia Britannica* went missing from the library's shelves. In January, Erika Bourgoin reported her purse stolen; three days later Sherri Long found it in the back seat of her husband's Ford. For three nights the poor man slept out at the Motel 6.

When we could wait no longer, we selected a committee. They would approach the Bynum house and knock on the door. Chief Allen would go, as would his one full-time officer, Big Joe Cobb—that much was obvious. They'd wear their uniforms, and the chief would keep his hand on his holstered .38, to show he meant business. Ed Night, who owned the gun range, would also go, along with his two grown sons. Martha Miller, the librarian, was a small woman, but she had a rapier mind and a razor tongue. She would do the talking.

Mark Lyles from *The Beacon* wanted to tag along, but that was roundly vetoed. He offered no real advantage to the group. If anything, his gout made him a liability. Though he was the closest thing to a journalist we had, he was prone to hyperbole. Any account he offered—in the event, say, he was the only one to return alive—would be unreliable at best.

There was talk of borrowing Kevlar vests from other municipalities, but what could protect a person from a child-witch who made you vomit feathers? What defense was there against the literally diabolical? (The discussion paused, in case Pastor Tripp spoke up to volunteer, but he stared at his wristwatch until talk started up again.) Martha would wear what she usually wore for a cold night out: a good long dress, comfortable shoes, a heavy cardigan. It was agreed. No vests, no helmets. Maybe a cross on a chain, though. (Again, we looked at Pas-

tor Tripp; again, he consulted his Timex.) Maybe garlic. Maybe a cherished letter or a lock of hair. The committee would fill their pockets with whatever charms and fetishes might curry courage.

We gathered at the pub on the chosen night. A new moon, we'd decided, though none of us could remember why. It was a Tuesday and we wandered in, one by one, after dusk, silently gathering around the tables. Rick O'Brien sat out among us instead of keeping his post behind the bar. By unspoken consensus, we left the row of barstools empty. They should be reserved, we sensed, for the committee's members.

Ed Knight and his boys were the first of them to arrive, six pistols between the three of them. They sat glumly, arms folded, on the three stools farthest from the door. Billy Knight—the younger brother who had played offensive line at the high school—was deathly pale and kept licking at its lips. (He wore a pink silk scarf tucked under his collar, but no one asked him why.)

Big Joe Cobb came next. He wore his full police uniform with its clattering black leather belt of gadgets and weapons. (Instead of his uniform black boots, though, he wore a pair of blue running shoes laced tight.)

Chief Allen and Martha Miller arrived together, with the chief holding the door for her. She seemed surprised—displeased, even—to see so many of us there. She scowled around the room imperiously, then seemed to gather where she was supposed to sit. She took the stool one over from Big Joe, so the Chief could sit by his officer.

For a good long while no one spoke. It was as if we were waiting for someone in charge to arrive, though we were all of us here. It was Rick O'Brien who broke the spell. He slipped behind the bar and lined up six shot glasses. He stood on tiptoe to reach a bottle on the highest shelf.

He nudged a slopping glass of it in front of each committee member.

Ed Knight and sons knocked theirs back right away, followed by the other two men. Martha Miller looked down at hers and then turned away, looking at the door instead. Big Joe, in his running shoes, reached behind the Chief and took her glass. He downed it without permission or apology. That seemed to do the trick. He licked his lips and stood.

So did the others.

So did we all.

We followed the six of them out to the sidewalk and watched them walk away, Martha in the lead and the others trailing her like geese. We watched until they turned down Gibson Street and were out of sight.

It was cold, and a wind was suddenly up, coming in damp from the lake. One by one we went back inside and sat. We left the barstools empty. The heater vent blew hot, dry air. It was so silent we heard the keg refrigerator heave off and on at intervals. Timbers creaked. Watches ticked. Pipes hissed overhead. We sensed that snow was beginning to fall outside. We waited, and we waited, and we waited. We waited much longer than seemed reasonable. We waited past all hope and purpose.

A little after two a.m., O'Brien edged over to the door and latched the deadbolt. He looked around at us, and we looked back at him. He unplugged the jukebox, and Gus Walker helped him push it in front of the door.

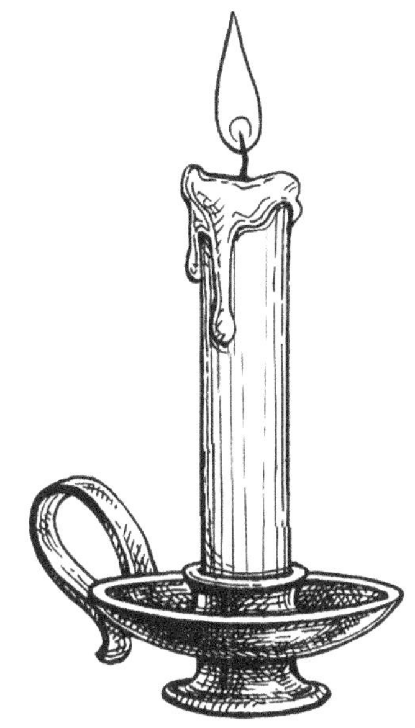

Delirus

by JP Relph

Margaret
January 1922

Ruth has been in the cellar again, despite our admonishments. Over these last four months she's become a different girl somehow. Gone is the abundance of joy, the mischief in her eyes – blue as the grape hyacinth that carpets the woods around our old house. Gone is much of her sweetness, her gentle nature, especially with her baby brother. This house was so filled with emptiness, with loss, when we came here; I find myself wondering if some of that settled in Ruth like spores.

She found a pram stored behind walls of old furniture. Hidden, I think. Thomas didn't note it when he moved some pieces down there. A doll inside, a little discoloured. We found Ruth, her beautiful black ringlets dust-aged, slumped in her bed with the monstrous thing. It is not a doll to hug during storms or invite to tea parties. A vile, grinning mouth with too many teeth encircles a hole that seems to whisper-howl. Painted squinting eyes, sour-apple green, and unfettered charcoal hair like mould blooming. Ruth calls the doll Delirus (she's been reading Latin – an obscure book the previous homeowner left behind). She won't be separated from the doll or the book, and has adopted something of the former's insolence in her eyes. The blue is somehow faded, cooled; the petals of the flower broken and browning.

February 1922

The doll was not a doll. Not just a doll. My daughter's eyes are pools of smashed ice. This house is splitting, revealing a doorway to madness.

March 1922

We are trapped here now. This is our red-brick tomb. Dear Thomas, always a phlegmatic man, has night-terrors, wakes weeping. He lost so much weight, so much *substance*, he seems wraithlike. Baby Arthur harbours a fungus in his frail chest that eludes treatment; he coughs incessantly. And what of me? I'm certain I feel my soul being dismantled by cold, porcelain hands. While the thing wearing my daughter like mourning weeds laughs and laughs.

-o-o-o-

Ava
January 2022

While my parents are off paint shopping, and Nanna's snoring contentedly on the sofa, I sneak into the cellar. The only place in this new-old house I've been warned to stay away from. They say it's really gross down there, toxic even, but I want to see for myself. I need to see. It's like an irritating toddler is gently tugging at my sleeve *come look, come look Ava*.

I open the door leading off the kitchen, pull the dangling switch and wait for two spotted bulbs to crackle to life. It's a rank-smelling space even from the top of the stairs. The light reveals fungus sliming every surface; the walls seem to lurch as I descend past them, the wooden stairs are

spongy, treacherous. More than once I feel my trainers losing grip, have to grab a curved handrail that's studded with oily-grey cups.

I step off onto a packed-soil floor, careful to avoid the clusters of fungi that seem horribly wet in the bulbs' weak glow. I see little mountains of bones in the corners of the small space – bird, rodent maybe. Creatures that somehow got trapped here, suffocated and desiccated. There's also the leathery curl of what was maybe a cat; it snarls at me with brown fangs. I'm guessing my parents thought that would upset me and that's why I was banned from here. It doesn't upset me - dead things rarely do – I'm more curious about the process, but the maybe-cat can wait. I've found something else.

Did it find me? Come look, come look Ava.

-o-o-o-

A mouldering pram with huge wheels pushed against the furthest wall. Tea-coloured crinkly lace around the hood, a mound of tatty blankets. The faded-navy outer fabric is striped with blister-like fungi; I try not to touch them as I peel the musty blankets back. Lean into underhood shadow, inhaling ancient dust and powdered insects.

A doll in a nest of scuffed satin, greets me with a demented toothy smile. I reel back a little, hear the squelch of something under my trainer. It's the grossest thing down here. Not soft, chipped pottery the colour of Nanna's smoking fingers. Once-black hair frizzing from beneath a knitted cap, scraps of ribbon rotting. Green eyes with lashes like scratches.

Ava, look.

I realise the mouth has an opening – perhaps for a tiny bottle with a teat – and from inside, something writhes, rustles. I reach a shivering finger, closer, closer still. My heart is painful in my chest, my breath scratchy, tasting of slime. Long legs are emerging from the dark hole, they probe the air around my fingertip, enwrap the doll's chapped lips like stitches. Pull.

I scream, fear-frozen when scrawny spiders heave themselves from the doll's foul grin. Hundreds of them. All have tiny porcelain faces with painted garish mouths and cruel eyes. Miniature versions of the thing they flood from. Hissing as one, they surge over my outstretched hand, up my arm. Wriggle into my open mouth before I can react, doll heads colliding like teeth clacking. I fall to my knees, scratch and scrape at my mouth with weak fingers. My heart is a ball of fire. My eyes roll until they fill with dirty-yellow bulb light. The final sensation, before a cold, almost welcome darkness overcomes me, is the itch-scrabble swarming of a thousand bristle legs inside my skull.

-o-o-o-

When I wake, I'm in the pram. Looking up at ratty lace, a murky slice of ceiling through painted eyes I can't close. It's unbearably cold. I can sense the spiders scrabbling about. Whatever presence inhabited the doll – *even as I think it, the name claws my mind: Delirus –*

piggybacked on the spiders, hijacked my body, which now sways next to the pram. I stare in horror as a maniacal grin stretches the slackened face white. My face, and not.

In returning to the spent doll, the spiders brought something of me with them. My consciousness, my soul maybe. If I believed in such things. It's impossible surely, but I have all my senses, ratcheted to the highest settings. I see my possessed body stumble away, Hear the slithering rip of fungi on the stairs. Then the lightbulbs pop like bones dislocating, I smell smoking dust, and the cellar turns pitch-black.

I think I'm screaming, but there's no sound, and besides, in this porcelain tomb, only the spiders, eagerly shroud-spinning, would hear. Nanna's screaming though, when it finally comes from two floors above me, it is cacophonous.

-o-o-o-

I don't know how much time passes before my body returns to the cellar. In the darkness I can only smell the sweat and blood when hands grab the side of the pram. At some point I hear it crumple to the ground. The spiders burst out of the doll like rotten seeds squeezed from a furred tomato. I hear that awful clicking as

they scramble and collide. For a moment I'm alone in the doll; an eternity of cold torture. When the spiders spill back in this time, it's with more than just the need for industrious web-spinning.

Ava, sweet Ava. You're not alone any-more.

I wait for the spiders to take me from this place – it's hot now, stuffy, like being completely wrapped in a sleeping bag – but they don't stop their work. I wait and wait, until the stench in the cellar ripens and I know I can never be returned. Later, there are heavy footfalls on the steps, the blaze of torches. I'm blinded by a wash of frigid-white light; the spiders' coil into the doll's deepest corners. I hear terrible wailing and realise it's my mother. Later still, the cellar door slams shut and screws are driven hard into wood.

The grotesque *thing*, my diabolical sleeping bag-mate laughs and, although I'm incorporeal in this doll-shaped coffin, I feel a tongue flick against my neck. A feverous, scarred body spoons me. The spiders wrap us in sheets of silver-grey, cocooning, and I weep. Weep until I'm dry as the doll herself and the *thing* licks my face raw.

-o-o-o-

Ava
January 1922

I wake to flickering candlelight. No, not wake - I haven't been in a peaceful slum-ber – more that I become aware of things outside the madness I reside in. The cellar is different; it smells of coal and musty furniture, but dry, clean.

The monstrous *thing* that knows all inches of me is animated. I feel a new fever inside the doll, an intoxicating delirium. It spreads like infection – I can taste it; syrup-sweet, my tongue reaches for it. The spiders are click-clacking as they surge up to the doll's mouth.

A face leers into view above me. Coils of dark hair feathered by dust. A girl, younger than me, excitement blushing her cheeks. She presses under the pram's hood, so close to the doll's face, her eyes are all I can see – a vivid blue, seeming full of flames. I know why she's here, how she was tempt-ed, called even, by a voice with no volume whispering like the turning of old pages.

Come look.

I'm moving. The candlelight comes and goes in brittle snatches. I see whitewashed brick, tall shapes covered in sheets, shelves crammed with jars. My cellar, and not. The girl has the doll under one arm; the spiders cling to the inside of its face. Stairs pass beneath us, small footprints in dust. The candle throws a shadow on the wall – a girl in a long frill-hemmed dress, stretched skinny.

As she climbs stairs, trails cellar dirt across polished wood and vibrant rugs, the *thing* shivers with impatience. Bangs blistered fists against the doll's insides; splinters of pottery fall like fine blades. I feel something of its urgency, its need. As if what is left of me now has corrupted. I guess I was always curious about the pro-cess of death. The syrup-sweet.

The girl climbs into a bed, rests the doll's head on the pillow so our eyes are again connected. She has thick lashes, beautiful, like spider legs, they droop and then close.

I hear hundreds of tiny doll heads chink like dainty teacups. I feel the *thing*, Delirus, pull me close. The girl's mouth opens a lit-tle as she starts to snore; I smell warm milk on her breath, unbrushed teeth. My heart is somewhere rotting, turned to brown mush, yet it strains against ribs, fills my head with crashing waves. Delirus whispers against my cheek, reeking of ash and bone marrow.

Come look, come look Ava.

We leave the doll in a squall of spiders and when Ruth opens those pretty blue eyes, I finally get to look.

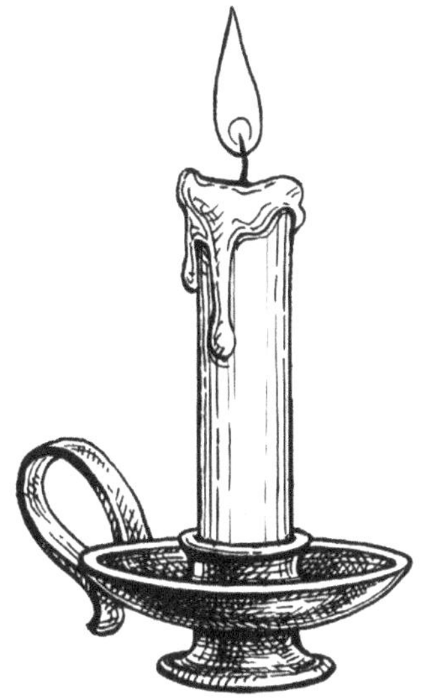

Living With It

by Reggie Chamberlain-King

*I*d idn't feel myself again until the dirt was tamped down and the earth washed from my hands

The water started to spiral in the plughole; it moved in a perfect screw, pulling the red and the brown in and down, sucking it all into the empty singularity in the middle. And then a familiar feeling rose inside me, a swirl in the belly, like agitated waters, churning over and over, draining away into the pit of my stomach and replenishing itself to start over – feeling just like my old self again, but, for a few moments there, I had been calm.

Anxiety feels first. It builds itself up inside of you, then it seeks a focus, a target, choosing a cause only after it's had an effect. The cause can be anything, the anxiety latches onto something. Only, now, for once, the cause was clear: the blood on my corduroy dress; the blood along the bathtub and twisting through the now-cold bathwater. And it felt no different justified than imagined, the same physical response.

I tore off the dress. I yanked out the plug. The water glugged away, the plughole choking it down in slow gasps... uuuahhh... It was all happening too slowly... uuuahhh... The pink water turned in large arcs about the fixture, but it was in no rush to disappear. I wanted to push it down, to force the water out and away from me. That desire translated itself into a painful wringing of the hands and

a scuffling of the feet as I watched the water haltingly recede... uuuahhh... slow gasps.

It had all been so quiet before: the splash... the strain... the words washed away by the water... they seemed muffled and far away. And I was serene, removed, floating above it. Couldn't feel my arms or legs. And when his head hit the white, rounded edge, it sounded like a bell rung in a distant church.

Now, the ceramic was still marked. The dress still bloodied. The water still sounded in the pipes... uuuahhh...

I opened the bathroom window easily, letting fresh air in to diffuse the heavy smell. My dressing gown – clean and dry; thick and warm – folded around me,

my hands digging into the deep pockets, searching for something…

The medicine cabinet… it opened easily too. There was a bottle of diazepam with my name on it – to be taken 2-4 times daily. Or as required. It depends on how you live with it. It's slow to take effect, maybe half an hour, and when it comes, when it descends on you, it is a heavy-limbed listlessness… the weight of dark wellwater is still in your stomach, but it is steady and stagnant, a slopping mass at rest. It slows you down to the speed of the rest of the world. It's not real calm, like those brief few minutes were.

The dress was fine for sopping up the blood that rimmed the bath… I could burn it later. Or bin it. The pills were already kicking in. A lot would have to wait until later. The heart still beats so fast, but, gradually, it's like your chest fills up with packing peanuts and the angst becomes a contained, quivering mass.

The dress went in the washing machine. I cleared away some of his toys; it shouldn't look like he's just been playing. But I didn't clear them all away, like he never played. He played. He made a mess. He screamed and roared as he tore around the house. And I put up with it, every cry, every tug of my leg, every trip, because he would tire himself out – he had to tire himself out eventually. He had to stop sometime. Somehow.

My arms began to drag and I fell into the armchair, its arms around me.

Again: contained, packed in, stowed away. The machine sloshed in the kitchen – the dress, the towels, with the drum wrapped round them. I imagined the water churning, running through the fibres; the blood coming out in tendrils, round and round, but never draining away.

Breathe slow, breathe easy.

It started raining, lightly at first, the gentle patter of tiny droplets. They spotted on the window. They fell onto the grass and on the earth. Brendan's shovel – the one I'd used - lay neglected on the lawn, fallen down dead. But the rain would wash it clean. And the rain would soften the freshly-turned soil and make it as one with the untouched dirt below, it all reduced to mud.

If the rain kept up, would it wash the mud away, uncovering something underneath?

If the rain kept up, I couldn't put the dress out on the line. It would have to go in the dryer. I'd throw some things in with it, to give the impression of a full load, for when Brendan came home.

If the rain kept up, my husband would be late. He would expect his dinner on the table then, the moment he walked in. He'd expect to kiss me on the cheek. To ruffle the hair of his best boy.

The rain kept up. I stayed in the armchair, feeling heavy and still.

"I don't know, love. He was just upstairs..."

There was a great weight on my chest. And on my eyelids.

"I don't know. I was just asleep for a minute... I don't know. Maybe two... three?"

I could have taken more pills and slept longer.

Brendan would understand though. He always said he knew how hard it was, that he wished he could be home more. He loved me, he said. He loved me more than the boy. He did. He does. I know it. He would know what to do... bury it

deeper... bury it further away. Cut it up. Burn it. He could do that sort of thing. He would make a plan. We would do it together. We would live with it, whatever happened.

And what happened was slow in coming.

Uuuahhh... the sound of water draining from the washer... patter patter... the sound of water on the window... the silent sound of water falling from my eyes into my hands.

I had the bottle of pills in the pocket of my dressing gown and I took another two. The dark water settled. It was the same feeling of relief and it was still. And it was still still after some time, but it was not calm, never calm. It was heaviness and the armchair took the weight of it. I fell asleep.

When Brendan woke me, the house was strangely quiet. The appliances had finished their cycles. The rain had stopped. I hadn't heard the key turn in the lock.

He smiled and I thought, "He understands." Although, I couldn't bring myself to speak before he said so himself.

"That explains it all," he said. "Poor mite."

And he tussled the hair of the boy that loitered shyly behind him – a mess of blond wet straggles stuck down across a gormless, white face.

"Poor love," said Brendan, as he leaned in to kiss me. "The door must have come off the snib behind him." Kiss. "No hat."

I shook my head – no hat.

The boy didn't look at me. His slick, dirt-smeared face stared ahead, as calm and unaffected as I felt. Then. He wore a red rain-slicker and he wore his green waterproof boots. His hands, all weather-beaten, were grey and they trembled.

"I'll order dinner, shall I?" asked my husband. "And we'll get you into the bath!" He meant the boy, who, yes, was foundered and dirty. And I thought about the bath. It was clean. And the dress was clean. And the shovel in the grass was clean.

His father took him up the stairs, in his little red rain-slicker and his little green boots, and I saw for the first time how dirty the boots were – thick mud around the soles and deep into the treads. The boy had left his mark across the floor: small, muddy footprints along the light carpet, out onto the bare wood of the hall. Through the window, I saw mud tracks continue along the garden path up to the edge of the lawn.

I opened the patio door and the air smelled wet and fresh. The mud tracks stopped where the grass began, but the grass was flattened, as though recently walked upon. It could have been me, I suppose - the indents ran off, past the fallen shovel, to the flowerbed at which I'd spent the afternoon digging and filling and weeping

His father joked with him, up in the bathroom. I heard Brendan through the open window. The boy didn't react though. Not a sound. I couldn't hear him laugh or shout, just his father's attempts to coax him into life... Nothing.

I put on my slippers and stepped out onto the dewy grass. If I found it was all a dream, it would be a relief. Anxiety feels first, then it finds its focus. It feels the same imagined or justified: a dark water, pooled or puddled in the pit of your stomach, black as mud or ditch-water.

And there it was. The rain had kept up, the soil turned to mud, and the torrent wore it away. The dirty water gathered in the palm of a child's upturned hand. Something of a cheek, a chin, an ear showed through the wetted earth.

I reached for the shovel and diligently filled the gaps in the grave. I would get on with it, whatever happened. I tamped down the dirt; the shovel fell to the ground. And I felt lighter, for once – or once again – lighter. And something in me rose, like the sound of boyish laughter that lifted up out of the bathroom window. Whatever it was, we would live with it.

The Other Door

by Rory Say

In every house I have lived in there has been a door that's kept locked.

Picture a plain white door in a house and you have seen it. Turn your head now and you might find its likeness nearby.

Only there are none just like it. Rarely does it remain in the same place for longer than a day. If I wake to see it in the wall past my feet, I am likely to come upon it later in some downstairs room, or in the hallway, and later again somewhere no door belongs—in the centre of a window, for example, or angled in the vaulted ceiling of a cramped attic. Often as a child I found it in the floorboards beneath my bed, under which I knew there was no basement.

Perhaps it was there when I first discovered it. I have memories of searching for toys beneath my bed and finding a door whose knob held fast when I tried to turn it. If I cried out for long enough, my mother or father would come blearily in. How many times did I watch their irritation shift to concern as it was explained to me, over and over, that there was no other door in the room? How long before I accepted that, from their point of view, they were telling the truth?

In terms of opening it, my earliest attempts were no more successful than my most recent ones. At first I used what methods were available; with fists and fingers I beat and clawed at the frame, until I was yelled at and punished for leaving dents and scratches on the walls throughout the house.

My continued fixation weighed heavily on my parents. They argued about what, if anything, was to be done with me. At last I was taken to a high room in a tall building, where a sharp-faced woman asked me questions about the other door. When did I first encounter it? Why did I think it was locked? What did I suppose lay on its far side?

But I did not wish to tell her these things. She had no right, I felt—and still feel now—to know them. So I stood from the chair and tried to leave, but the knob on the door behind me wouldn't budge when I clutched it, and I screamed as I beat and clawed at the frame.

The situation at home, bad as it was, worsened in the wake of this incident. I could no longer bear the thought of a locked door—*any* locked door—in the house. All were to be kept open, preferably ajar. This meant that every night it was necessary to creep from bed and open the front door, which was the only one that my father, no matter how I pleaded, insisted be kept shut and locked.

I was routinely punished for doing this and yet I kept doing it, and the fact I kept doing it, as well as the increasing severity of the punishments inflicted upon me (there was, I recall, some disagreement as to the nature of these punishments), deepened the rift that divided my parents. An unpleasant rivalry ensued, as each sought privately to poison my view of the other. At the same time, my wellbeing was daily and loudly debated as though I myself were not present, and I began to feel only partly visible, a bystander in my own skin, there and not there, like the other door through which I could never escape.

We moved houses. Or rather my father moved while my mother stayed where we had been. Though fearful of moving anywhere, I was obliged to spend every Wednesday and Sunday night at this different house of my father's, which was really only part of a house, with fewer doors that locked. Nevertheless, it was there I learned that the other door followed me. In the morning after I had spent my first night in the house, I found it waiting in the living room, behind the couch on which my father still slept.

As I wedged myself between the couch and the wall, he awoke and asked me what in the world I was doing. I paused with my hand on the knob, but before I could think of how to explain, I saw that look on my father's face I had grown so deeply to fear.

Next I was taken to a group of men who took blood from my arms with needles and tubes, and who placed a helmet on my head so they could study my brain. For some reason, these measures brought out the worst in my parents, who more adamantly than ever refused to share a house.

Then came a Sunday when I was dropped off to stay with my father and found nobody there to meet me. Was some sort of game in play? Nothing could be more uncharacteristic of my father, whose idea of play was that it should always be structured and essentially educational.

So I sat down on the bed that was his when I was gone and mine when I was there and awaited his return.

How long did I wait? I suppose, in a way, I am still waiting now.

When I grew too frightened of the empty quiet, I went to leave the room but froze in the doorway as though I'd been struck. Suddenly I felt watched, or keenly perceived in some other way. Turning around, I knew just where I would find the other door.

On the opposite side of the bed, half hidden past my father's collection of hanging shirts, I could see it in the closet. There was no mistaking what it was, and yet some indefinable change drew me across the room. Only after I had pushed aside what clothes were in the way could I clearly see the translucent, skin-like laminate that now covered every inch of the door's frame.

The search for my father commenced that very night, and continues, at least in some official capacity, to the present. I have been told that the strains of a troubled child can at times be too great a burden for a parent to bear; too irresistible becomes the temptation to flee when the opportunity presents itself, resettle somewhere, and keep guilt buried as deep as can be.

But why is it that I have trouble believing he is really, entirely gone? I have never felt his absence so strongly as does my mother. For in every house I have lived in there has been a door that's kept locked, one whose white frame now pulses with a warm, pleasant heat, as though it were a body that had spent all its days in the sun.

PENCE
TEN
10

Coin, Mirror, Manoeuvre

by Mark Blayney

I live in the woods. A running brook behind the house so it's never quiet; the sound is comforting. My home has seven rooms, all mostly empty.

There's a stove, with one working hob – the oven and other hobs are lifeless, and I'm not brave enough to investigate the gas pipes and see if it can be fixed. I wouldn't get to sleep for worry it might kill me in the night.

What do I eat? Well, you get by. I can fish. Downhill it's a twenty-minute walk to the road and sooner or later you find a bit of roadkill. There was a pheasant once, the meat untouched, the truck tyre impression across its crushed head. Lovely.

Always trucks. These days there are no other vehicles. You hear them in the night, prowling.

Late August, the lanes weighed down with blackberries. I take plastic takeaway tubs from the before-times to use for foraging. A grey rucksack with a penknife in it, for mushrooms and whatever, and the tubs stacked inside each other like transparent Russian dolls. When filled with fruit, I take a random lid and seal the top. You have to press on one side and then the next and then the next and then the next and then the next and eventually it decides, okay, I will stay closed.

I fill a third pot of blackberries and perform the lid dance. Long ago, this one was prawn biryani. Near the blackberry bush is a plum tree. Three out of four are rotting now, yellow pus-coloured fruits with sugary globules erupting from them, but I can pull the higher branches down and fill two tubs. Chicken Makhani. Beef korma.

I see – just a glimpse – a man at the edge of the woods. My surprise is rapidly overtaken by a frown. The strange thing is, he looks quite a lot like me, the impression emphasised by the fact he has a grey rucksack.

There's the man again. A sighting between trees, a grey flash like a man-sized squirrel. He turns, sees me and smiles. I find myself smiling back. I don't want to, I want to glare at him. This is my patch. The rabbits and pheasants are for me.

He really does look very similar to me. I suppose this is not as surprising as it might seem. I've got a very common head. All over buzzcut, or I'd have tufts of hair at the side. Undistinguished eyebrows, saggy jaw, plain bland face, everything a bit too small for the skin. I run a hand over this rough head – I am conserving the trimmer. There's still some life in my twenty-settings shaver, but it can't last much longer. Electricity – take it for granted all your life. I fear the day the gas pipe to the cooker cuts off. It's probably feeding off the guard installations, and my usage is so small

they don't notice. No water, of course. Fortunately the brook runs cheerfully itself. They say you can't invent a perpetual motion machine. Have they never looked at a river?

I used to be a – well, doesn't matter what I used to be, does it? Doesn't matter what any of us used to be. The point is, this guy, the same build and nondescript clothes, could be me, inhabiting the wrong universe.

Or maybe he's inhabiting the correct universe, and it's me in the wrong one. How would you tell?

'Hello,' he says, heading over. For some reason I didn't expect him to speak. 'What are the chances?'

'Well yeah. Unlikely.'

He nods, and I can't help it, I nod back.

'You've come at last.'

'No, I always come this way. Unless I go the other way.' I point along the brook.

He shakes his head. Tosser. I shake my head. I'll show him.

'Come with me,' he says.

'Why?'

He's already leading the way and now glances back, momentarily confused. 'Well,' he considers, furrows his unfurrowed brow.

'I've got something to show you,' he says, after far too long a pause.

Not interested. He beckons me. I beckon him. 'Come to mine,' I say, 'then perhaps next time I'll come to yours.'

He doesn't shrug, doesn't react. Just turns, with a kind of *oh well your loss* expression.

I emit a soundless sigh, if such a thing is possible. Then I follow him.

I've had no company for months. You would as well. Wouldn't you?

Well, it's too late now. Don't worry, nothing terrible happens. At least I don't think it does. To be honest, I can't tell any more.

The layout is identical to mine but that's no surprise, all the houses round here were built to the same plan. Two modest but not cramped rooms, hallway at the side. I can see through the knocked-out doorway that he has a single-storey extension at the back, which I don't have. He's turned this into a kitchen. Much better than my pokey old place.

'What did you want to show me?'

He hovers, removes his jacket. Like mine but not as battered. He lifts his eyebrows in a pointing direction. 'Upstairs.'

I raise my eyebrows in surprise. He leads the way. I wait in the hallway, hand on the banister. Polished wooden stairs. Much better kept than mine. You can almost see yourself in them. I take the first step then change my mind and head back to the entrance. Before leaving I take a wistful look into the front room. Bookcase with books. Picture. Coffee table. Rug. Old times.

Too comfortable. I pull up my collar, like I'm a close-up of me in a film, and head out silently, the door ajar. The freshness of the path, the greenery, the first coolness of autumn. A tree with red leaves forming. I take a lungful of beautiful air. They can't take that away from us, can they? Although they did try.

He leans from an upstairs window. 'What are you doing?' He has my frown, my hunch of a shoulder.

I frown. 'Going home.'

'Why?'

'Because I want to.'

'Then you won't see what I've got to show you.'

'Don't care.' It's like we're children.

'It's good.' Now he's palming the side of his chin in the way I do.

I don't reply but rub my chin thoughtfully and head off.

Salmon. I'd like to learn how to smoke it. I imagine the fish in silver foil, baking slowly. In this fantasy it flaps its tail despite being dead and its milky eye studies me forlornly.

I'm proud to have caught it but chopping into small pieces and boiling it won't really cut the mustard. Mustard. Old times.

How do you smoke something? You get bits of wood, don't you, and hang the fish up, and then you put flames underneath, and it needs to be in a small dry room, doesn't it, a smokehouse. What could I convert for that purpose? The outhouse, I guess, if it's dry enough.

Fresh pail of water from the brook; put the salmon on a plate; sit it on the bucket to keep cool; then put it in the coldest part of the house, the cupboard under the stairs, where bobbles of damp-pushed paint blister the walls.

I weigh up the outhouse's possibilities. It's a strange building. Too small to be an outside toilet. No idea what it was for. Glossy black door, now peeling heavily. A sloped metal roof, guttering pulling away. Someone's tried to do a quick fix by nailing things back into place but now the nails are coming off as well, one dangling like a raindrop, suspended for years perhaps. There's probably asbestos in there but that's the least of my troubles.

Getting the door open means flattening long grass and weeds and pulling out some resistant thistle. Inside, incongruously, it has been wallpapered. Yellow, with faded teddy bears; left over from the nursery I suppose. In those days, like now, you never threw anything away. If they had a strip of wallpaper left, they'd look round for somewhere to use it.

A small mirror hangs at the back. Why would you need a mirror in there? Is it for seeing what's behind you? Or again, perhaps the owners of this house, whoever they were, had a mirror, and had to hang it somewhere. I don't remember it, but that doesn't mean it wasn't always there.

The mirror like everything else is old, mottled with brown spots, the silvering long gone from the edges. I rub my chin. The structure looks promising. You can do this, I convince myself. But not in time for the fish on the plate on the bucket under the stairs. It will have to be boiled. I really need to fix the oven.

'Please come in.'

'I just thought after last time...'

'It's fine.' He smiles. 'I was just about to eat. Join me if you like.'

I smile back. 'No of course not. I...'

But he's retreated into the gloom of the hallway and I follow. I can't smell cooking. In the back room he has salad, beans, berries.

Where my fireplace is, his is boarded up. Why would he do that?

'How can I help you?' He eats a radish.

'I wondered if you had some tools I could borrow.'

'Of course. What's wrong with it?' He takes a forkful of beans, and my mouth waters in response.

'With what?'

'The oven. Is it the gas pipes?'

'How do you know?'

'You told me last time.'

I didn't. My face communicates this information.

'You were down here, and you were talking to yourself. You don't want to have to fix it solo.' He pops a carrot baton in his mouth. 'Don't worry. I'll come round and help.'

'I don't want to put you to any trouble.' My words sound stiff, unnatural.

Slice of apple, or is it beetroot. 'No trouble. Although...'

'Yes?'

'The deal is, you let me show you what I wanted to last time.'

'All right.'

He smacks his hands together, then

rubs them excitedly. We are all short on company here. He bounds up the stairs two at a time.

On the landing, in the corner where I have a linen cupboard, there's a high, narrow table set up somewhat artificially, with a stool behind it and another in front. It's covered in black cloth and there's a red box with silver foil moons and stars.

'You do tricks?'

He lifts his shoulders and grins. 'Care to take a seat?'

I shrug, and pretend to grin in response.

He levers himself in behind the table. 'Okay.'

From underneath – there must be a shelf or something – he produces a hand mirror. He flexes his fingers, in that way magicians do to show they're not hiding anything, which they are. Holds the mirror vertically on the table and beckons me to sit down.

'Have you got 10p?'

Of course not. No one has coins any more. But when I stick my hands in my trousers to prove it, a coin emerges glimmering in my palm like a stone from a river. Silently I hand it over.

'Good. Now watch.' He places the coin in front of the mirror. 'Don't take your eye off it.' He slides it along. As it reaches the edge of the rectangle, the reflection appears to slide out with it. Now there are two coins, the shield the right way up, where mine is upside down.

He motions me to take them. He does it again. The two coins slide along, then two new coins appear behind the mirror.

'Again,' he murmurs with concentration. This time I have to help. Together we slide the four coins along. Four reflections turn into coins.

'There you go. A profitable morning.'

'How do you do it?'

It's obvious how he does it – you

have the other coins behind the mirror, and when you slide the front one out, you bring the hidden one out alongside it. I didn't see the other coins before the trick; but that's what magicians do, isn't it? Palming things, making them seem to appear out of thin air when they were there all along.

The coins all have the same newish quality; still shiny, but not mint.

'So how do you do it?'

'I'll tell you.' He leans in, looks to either side of me. 'I cheat.'

Right. 'That's really what you wanted to show me?'

Spreads his hands wide. 'I don't have anyone else to show.'

I look at my palms, as if expecting the coins to have disappeared. They're still there.

He jumps up. The doors to the bedrooms are closed. He has a carpeted staircase, leading to the loft – he must have another room up there, whereas I just have a ceiling, and a hatchway, and a nothingness, that I never use. Why would you need it? Something jolts me as I think this, makes me want to go home and look.

I take a sly look at my financial gain. The coins have the same year running around the king's head: 2023. You won't remember 2023, you're too young.

'So.' He turns to me. 'You want your oven mended.'

His legs poke out from underneath. Banging, clattering. I stand and watch uselessly.

He pulls himself out, a smear of oil on his face. 'Done.'

'Really?'

The way he studies me it crosses my mind that he's done something with the pipes so they'll kill me in the night after all. I am competition for resources, let's face it.

It's just the grease on his face, giving

him the strange look. I show him out. As a joke I try to pay him with two or three of the coins, but he takes them seriously and nods.

In the hallway he looks at the picture on the wall. 'Your wife?'

'Yes.'

'She died?'

I nod.

'Mine too.'

'I'm sorry.' I close the door behind him with a satisfying click.

That evening I eat well. The house smells homely. The gas seems to run fine. I open the last wine bottle and toast the pipe – keep working, keep working. Already it is dark at 7 and I have nothing to do other than go to bed. There are probably some candles in the drawers, I can't remember. I will use them if we reach November.

I'm restless in bed, too hot and too cold at once. I wake up wanting water. It's 3-ish. Owls, foxes, badgers. No way can I sleep through this racket. The countryside is bloody noisy, I long for the peace of a city.

Downstairs I take a suspicious look at the oven. It seems to be okay.

Overcoat over pyjamas, I latch the door and head up the path. It must be nearer 4, because the faintest blue light helps me navigate. Even so I trip on some snaky branches on the way. His house has no lights, but why would it? He won't have electricity any more than I have.

But I'm confident he's asleep. His front door is stiff but opens, without the horror-film creak I expect. The large hallway mirror reflects the indigo sky enough for me to make out the staircase. It should be simple, being the same layout as my own; but even in your own house everything is different at dead of night.

The table is still set up for the trick. My eyes accustomed to the dark now. The little silver moon and stars on the red box shine dimly at me. Stupidly, I realise I'm not wearing the same trousers as before. Have I really come all this way for nothing? But, in my pyjama pockets, there's a 10p coin.

A lozenge of blue light on the table shapes itself into the hand mirror and I draw it to me, lining it up perpendicularly as he did. Peculiar word, perpendicularly. Perhaps I've just made it up. Before trying the trick and disappointing myself, I realise it won't work in this seat. I need to be on his side. The chair scrapes when I pull it forward. Everything's much louder at night, isn't it? Apart from the things that are quieter.

I sit perpendicularly and place the 10p in position. I glance over the top as he did; not only does the magician never reveal the trick to the punter, he never reveals it to himself. I slide the coin along. As it reaches the edge, its reflection – unclear because it's so dark – emerges alongside. Two coins on the table.

They're both quite solid. I compare them. I could keep doing this – I would be rich. I remember, vaguely, thinking this as a child. How could I have thought that?

I lay the mirror flat, quietly; but it's as loud as the crack of a pop gun.

It's dawn as I reach my house, and it feels as if I've been travelling all through the night. Maria will still be asleep, and baby Noah too. For a moment it's as if I didn't have a child – it takes a while to remind yourself sometimes. It takes a long time to sink in. Being alive hasn't sunk in yet, really. I remember a few years ago we travelled in the desert – Egypt or Jordan, I can't remember the country. When the sky goes from horizon to horizon it ceases to be the sky – it's too large to be anything to name.

I unlock the door, listen to the house breathe around me. Switch on the lights. I can smell last night's dinner. Opening the fridge I see Marie has put leftover dinner in there. Wine. Treats. My favourite cherry pie – expensive, from the shop round the corner, but worth it.

It is bracing to walk at night. You come home a different person. I empty my pockets. A lock of Noah's hair and some 10p coins.

Maria will be up soon. She always was an early riser, even before Noah was born, so I do not worry too much about being noisy. After she's done the first feed I will take over, lying on the sofa with Noah on my lap until I fall asleep. I can't remember now why I was out so late, but so what. A nocturnal walk is good for the soul. Through the hatch we've knocked through – the latest thing, Marie says all our neighbours have done it – I see the curvy rectangle of the TV, greyly looking at me. Strange word, greyly. Perhaps I've just made it up. I rub my chin.

Do you ever have that feeling when you're in your own house that you're not really there? That your brain is five minutes behind your body, or is it the other way round? In a moment of fear I head up the stairs. But it's fine. I can hear Maria breathing behind the closed door and if I listen carefully, there are Noah's shorter, faster, higher breaths as well. I lean my head against the solid wood. All you need in life is for things to be solid. Not predictable, that would be boring. But you do need reliable.

I glance at the three walls of the landing. It's as if there's something missing. The hatchway, to the loft. Let's do something with that – turn it into a playroom. Yes, for when Noah's older.

I take the bag of nappies from the doorway and head down the path. We're using the old coal shed for the bins – seems a happy arrangement and keeps the garden tidy. I didn't even know what the coal shed was until someone explained it to me. The yellow paper, the teddy bears. I suppose it's whoever owned the house before us, or the owners before them, or before them.

We talk about 'owning houses'. No. The houses own us; we are their temporary keepers. I stand up, knees suddenly creaky. I look in the old cracked mirror. The face is not me. It's an old man. How can it be an old man, when I am just a child?

Back in the house, the furniture has shifted. The view down to the woods makes me nervous. They have told us not to go down there. They've said it's unsafe – I think there's been some terrible devastation, a war perhaps. Something they're not telling us.

In the night I hear the trucks. I ask for a drink, but no one pays attention. I can hardly move. These pyjamas are so uncomfortable. Please may I have a drink now?

Let me do the trick for you. I used to do this trick as a child, then when I was an adult – in the before-times – for my son, Noah. He loved it. He wanted more, more, more.

Get everyone else to gather round, they'll want to see it. Here, sit opposite me. May I have a drink now? I'm thirsty. Don't go. Please don't go.

The Catafalque

by Victoria Dowd

The small cemetery chapel had never been home to anyone but the dead. Tied with ivy to its woodland bed; fallen into disuse.

A Victorian idea of Gothic beauty, ornate stained glass and finely carved arches, it was sealed up after the last funeral. This was 1953, people preferred something less formal, a nice crematorium.

It was a mean, cold dusk and the granite sky cast a maudlin light over the stones as th e new inhabitants, the Bradwells, picked their way through the muddy cemetery path, not stopping to read any of the inscriptions on the gravestones or peer through the cracks in the crumbling sarcophagi.

No-one used the gate anymore. It was for the coach and horses, the estate agent had said, but such grandeur had fallen from favour now death had become more functional.

The skeletons of trees bent low round the gable end of the chapel, holding the building close, protecting it or hiding it. There was an old tower which had housed the bell, silenced in the war and taken years ago. At the base of it was the thick oak door, studded with black iron and laced in with black hinges.

Mr Bradwell took out a sturdy key and paused. A soft wind touched his cheek. A single black rook sat on a post, watching.

'You scared me,' he breathed. 'Silly bird.'

Mrs Bradwell turned to where the bird sat, its black marble eyes watched her, reflecting the splintered fingers of the trees.

'Go on, shoo.' Mr Bradwell waved his hand sharply.

The rusted key fell to the stone with one dead sound and the startled bird wheeled into the sky in a splash of silver black wings. But the nagging feeling he was being watched had not left with the bird.

As he bent down to pick up the key, amongst the cover of tired old leaves, he observed something on the stone porch floor. Footprints. He touched their small outline. They were dainty feet.

'What's this?' he murmured.

'Kids playing where they shouldn't?' Mrs Bradwell offered.

They looked bigger than that. Teenagers most likely getting up to things in the cemetery. Mr Bradwell drew back the leaves. The footprints seemed to go into the chapel, and the last one was cut clean in half by the door. They had not worn any shoes.

Mr Bradwell stood, holding the cold, heavy key. The timeworn door was tired and scratched deep with gouges that mapped out years of neglect. A sudden flurry of wind sent leaves spiralling up. He gripped the key and, quick as fear, turned it in the lock.

The door was stiff as he dragged it back across the stones. Inside was desolate, the spent air hanging above long vacated pews. The sharp, mildewed smell of dust blew in their face. Rows of dark wood stood like children's abandoned desks. Dusk's grey light fell in shafts across the bone white stones. The occasional small pane of glass was shattered allowing a pinprick view out but there was no broken glass on the floor inside.

Everything was as if the last eulogy had been read and the mourners had filed out locking the door behind them. Perfectly preserved in that last, dead moment of grief, it had been sealed away from the world.

Stained glass saints watched their steady progress along the aisle. How many mournful processions had they looked down on? Some raised their eyes to heaven as if to avoid the sadness below.

It would need a lot of work to see the light of potential in this darkness.

Shadows drew closer as the day began to fail. Mr Bradwell pulled his thin coat round himself.

Cough.

He stopped. His eyes, searching the dank gloom, landed on the most dramatic of the windows, the Virgin with great, faded rays of celestial light. A rainbow of light bled out towards a thick wooden platform - the old catafalque where the coffins would rest. He'd seen one used at a funeral. This one had a dark veneer that caught the dull light. Mrs Bradwell stepped towards it, seeing her own reflection in its varnish. The air had a dark, mineral edge to it now.

'Garden Chapel,' Mr Bradwell said. That's what they'd call it.

She made no objection. His wife, Emily had always been the shy sort but hid it well behind a studious air of contemplation.

It was Mr. Bradwell who'd first seen

the For Sale board. A quiet, solemn man, he'd been something in the war. Everyone had been something in the war. But in the real world, he was an architect so he could see the potential here. Mid-forties, respectable, and his job gave him contacts and ideas. This would be a great project for him to get his teeth into. It would be a sensitive conversion, very much in keeping with the area, he'd told the estate agent. He and his wife once lived nearby but she'd not been terribly well. Her nerves.

Emily studied the stained glass. She never minded him talking about her like that. People had done it a lot – Mark, doctors, friends, all so worried. It had been a worrying time.

An uncomfortable air clouded the church like incense. They walked, heads bent, along the aisle.

Garden Chapel would be a new chapter, a fresh start and lots of words the doctors had said Emily needed. It would take time, they'd said. Some people just had sensitive souls.

The work, as with all these respectful projects, was swift and brutal. Great whirls of dust veiled the sky above the chapel. Rather than breathing new life into the building, it seemed like they were punching it out of the old stones. No one came to visit, steering clear of this invasion.

Garden Chapel was ready after Christmas and Mark opened a bottle of claret to celebrate. He'd put it away since they were married so it seemed appropriate to open it now. He nursed his glass as Emily sat opposite him at the candlelit table.

'To us,' he smiled.

'To us, my darling,' she replied.

She patted the table. 'This was a marvellous idea of yours.'

He pushed his glasses back up his nose modestly.

'Who would have thought of using this as a table? A coffin's platform,' she said grandly.

He sat back and folded his arms across his chest.

'Sorry,' she held up her hand, 'a catafalque, I know. You're a very clever man and this is a remarkable table.'

She ran her finger around the rim of the wine glass.

He surveyed the room and raised his glass. 'To new beginnings. Not too morbid all this, I hope.' He was used to reading the signs.

'God, no! I love it. You've done a marvellous job. It would be wrong to wipe it all away. Everything has a past.'

She watched as he blindly stared at her. She could see him wishing he could just walk inside her head and find all the answers. But like the doctors said, such things were complicated and sometimes had no reason. It was all a question of time. There it was again - time, stalking around him, waiting.

'Mark, it's amazing. *You're* amazing.'

She held his hand and looked at him closely.

Garden Chapel was designed to the highest degree. The pews had been moved round the new table, some had been upholstered to create sofas. A kitchen had been installed where the old chaplain's office was, and had all the mod cons, even a Kenwood mixer. The stained glass was cleaned and up-lit. Even the lectern had been preserved but in place of a Bible there was a photograph of their wedding that Emily gave him on their first anniversary. It was a unique and sensitively renovated project, exploring the boundaries of what could be achieved with a challenging space. At least, that's what Mark said.

After the breakdown, she needed solitude and there was a lot of that here. When Mark was at work, she watched the mourners who came to the graves. She spent hours looking at the people who walked through the gardens, sometimes with dogs, sometimes alone with their thoughts. They occasionally glanced at the chapel, stealing a quick look. Emily might have been imagining it, but she could have sworn people increased their step, huddled deeper into their coats and looked down.

Emily didn't go out much. She didn't work. During the war she'd been in coding but her nerves weren't stable enough for that now. Fragile was a word she'd heard a lot. She tried to keep things on an even keel for Mark. He'd been through so much. So she always took the tablets the doctors gave her and let the tears fall when he was at work.

Monday came around again with its usual regularity. She kissed Mark and said not to worry, she'd be ok.

The chapel was vast and empty when he'd gone. A whole room of silence. She started to clear away breakfast. Smoothing down the blue silk cloth on the table, her hand paused. She frowned. It felt warm like a bed after a night's sleep. Her head fell to the side and she studied the large wooden table. Catafalque, that's what he called it – a beautiful word for such a solemn object. There was no way they could have thrown it away and this seemed like such an elegant use for it. She lifted the cloth. The surface was glossier, with a freshness none of the other wood in the chapel had. There was a solid curve to it as if it had been hewn from a single tree. Emily ran her hand tenderly along its grain, feeling every knot and indent. She held her hand on its soft facade. The warmth seemed to radiate from it. Natural materials, Mark had said. Hold your hand to any great wooden structure, it stores its own ambience.

Cough.

She fell back on her heels and looked around the empty cavern of the room. The lights blazed as usual, and the stained glass shone down on her. She was alone. And yet, it didn't feel like that.

She let the blue silk cover fall back.

Mark was a busy flurry as always

when he arrived on the stroke of six. She'd spent the last hour fluffing cushions and moving vases to make it seem more like home. Emily smiled as soon as he came through the door, so he knew not to worry. She didn't mention that she felt like she was being watched; that she thought someone was spying on them, she just said, 'Hello darling, how was your day?'

That night, she lay in the large, ornate bed staring into the dark tower above. Mark slept soundly beside her; and the room peaceful. Her eyes drifted and her thoughts began to settle. The feeling of calm and stillness was a relief to her tangled mind. She was vaguely aware of a small, lulling sound, a repetitive long note in the back of her thoughts. It rang again, slowly, and again, becoming more insistent until her eyes flicked open. It was a bell ringing.

She sat up and looked into the shadows of the tower. The slow, rhythmic tone echoed through the darkness. A constant, single note. She flicked on her side light but could see no further up the tower. Mark stirred beside her, forever alert to her nightmares as if he had adopted them as his own.

'Is that you?' his voice was gruff with sleep.

'Yes,' she whispered. 'I'm fine. Go back to sleep.'

The bell had slowed into a stop and now there was only the distant sound of the wind. Emily waited in the darkness until she finally succumbed to exhaustion.

Mark left before she woke. The fresh, cool sunlight flooding the room below seemed to lift her troubled thoughts. She descended the new spiral staircase and breathed in the heady, warm air. It smelt different today, a sweet fragrance but with a strange earthy edge to it. As she moved towards the dining area, it grew stronger. It was a cloying, fungal smell that verged on decay. The smell hung over everything with a lethargic weight, sinking into her clothes, her hair. As she drew nearer, it was almost unbearable. She felt nauseous breathing the foetid air.

The scent was at its strongest by the table, like rotting flowers in a vase. Yes, that was it! It was identical to the memory of flowers left until the water turns brackish. Lilies were her favourite and this did smell remarkably like the moment they turn. But there were no flowers in the house. The table was clear.

And then the smell was gone.

It didn't fade. It disappeared as if it had never been there. The windows were shut and the air hadn't moved. The stale odour had simply vanished as if she'd imagined it.

That wasn't a thought she should have let in. She went to the kitchen and opened the cupboard. Her pills. Emily was told if there was any possible hint of her previous anxieties she must immediately take the medication. They weren't there. She checked another cupboard, then another. She'd brought them with her, she must have.

Scratch.

She swung round, the blood flushed faster through her veins. Sweat beaded on her temples and yet she felt that familiar cool breeze flowing through the room.

Scratch.

The small, sharp sound raked against something solid. It grew louder, more insistent; rapid little scratching sounds. Mice. Rats even. The building was old, the cemetery unkempt. She'd have to get someone in. She bent to listen at the floorboards but the sound was coming from the main room.

She walked carefully, looking for any unwelcome little visitors in the corners. The scraping grew louder, faster. It seemed to echo in the cavernous room. It was digging deep into the wood, tearing against the grain.

Her eyes settled on the catafalque. The blue satin cloth lay undisturbed, but as she drew closer the ravenous clawing sound grew louder as if the wood was being gouged away. She placed her ear against the smooth wood.

Thump.

Emily fell back. Another strong, low thud. Then another. Faster, until there was a great thunder within the vast catafalque. Emily stared at the wood. Each corner seemed to vibrate with the drumming as if something was... inside.

She touched the smooth surface again. It was warm. The catafalque was solid. She knew that. There couldn't be anything inside. There was nothing under the solid stone floor. She wiped the sweat from her face and tried to calm the fluttering in her chest. She felt sick. Sour water pooled behind her teeth.

Her heart rippled. She clutched her hands together and closed her eyes, willing it to go away. Then her eyes sparkled over with violet black.

☠

Emily didn't know how long she had been lying there but shadows had started to climb up the corners again. She wiped her hand across her mouth. She remembered the scratching but now there was only silence. In the grey half-light, the room seemed almost set into the stone, petrified in a moment. The catafalque sat in the bruised glow of the stained glass.

She moved as if her feet might break the old stones. The catafalque seemed to glow with the silver sheen of the blue satin. But the material wasn't smooth now. It was bunched in places crudely, as if it had been grabbed.

There was a very familiar pattern to the curves. Long smooth lines were drawn up into silver white shapes, hollows formed between them. She followed the creases and folds until she came to the rounded form at the very top.

A head.

There under the fine cloth lay the unmistakable outline of a body. Slim and still in the cool, dark light, the limbs lay shrouded.

Emily's mouth fell slack, her chest gathered in fear.

'This is not real,' she whispered. 'This is not real.' She repeated it over and over like a mantra. 'This is your mind.' Emily looked at the perfect mould of a human and felt the overwhelming urge to touch it. She reached out. The only light in the room now was the catafalque. The rest had fallen into darkness. Her fingers almost touched the silk when she saw the dark stain bloom out across the material. The figure was bleeding.

No, she was bleeding. She looked down at her hands. The knuckles torn and raw. She turned her hand and saw nails missing, deep lacerations down the fingers.

'I'm losing my mind,' she held her hands either side of her head. Slowly, she climbed onto the catafalque, and in perfect imitation of the form below she sank onto the smooth surface. She lay there on the new bed, feeling the comfort swill through her, drifting into the warm arms of the wood. And she slept in the darkness on top of the catafalque.

She had not slept like that in years. It was the sort of sleep she remembered from childhood. Uncomplicated, passive sleep where she didn't fight it; it came as naturally as breathing. When she woke, she felt a sense of thankfulness for the peaceful, tender hours she'd regained.

But where was Mark? It was dark now, the sky seeded with stars. He should have been home hours ago. The bell was ringing the hour. She counted: eight, nine, ten. Ten o'clock. Something was wrong. He hadn't said he'd be late.

She slowly climbed down from the catafalque, wrapping the blue silk cloth around her. It was cold and the lights were out.

She ran to the door and looked out. The wind sailed round the house, whipping the branches and twisting them in towards the chapel.

'Mark?' She shouted. 'Mark?' She ran out into the dark air. The cemetery was desolate. No one came here at night. The old iron gate swung on its hinges.

'Mark?'

She ran with the blue silk trailing behind her high on the waves of the wind. She didn't see the stone. She didn't feel the fall.

Emily lay sprawled in the dirt, a river of blue silk around her. She turned her head to see the broken stone, choked with ivy. Her eyes widened in horror. She scrambled forward and her bloody fingers traced over the carved letters. Emily Bradwell 1914-1951 wife of Mark Bradwell.

The ground was soft and uneven beneath her, portions of soil had fallen inwards. She scrabbled frantically, her fingers tearing, nails splintering as they had done before. She gouged out great sections of the soil. She felt the air thin in her throat, the wooden sides of the coffin against her arms. She saw the unending darkness smothering her as the bell rang. There'd been no bell for years the agent had said.

☠

'A unique property,' the estate agent told the young couple.

The woman pulled a face. 'My mother told me the bloke there killed his wife.'

The estate agent sighed and put the details down. 'He was punished for his crime. Found him lying on her grave, mad as a hatter and when they dug her up. She'd been drugged and buried alive a couple of years ago.'

There'd be no sale today.

The Resurrection Man

by Eve Chancellor

*I*knelt closer to the cadaver, shining my candle over its waxy moon-like face, squinting to get a good look at the victim's identity one last time.

We'd left no bruises, nor blows to the head. The lad's eyes were closed, as if he were merely sleeping. He couldn't have been much older than fourteen, his face the emaciated mask of poverty. He didn't smell of the grave.

'How'd you come about a Thing so fresh?' the corpse-hauler asked, lowering his voice to just above a sneer. His face was pale with hollow cheeks, small wire-rimmed glasses pinching the tip of his nose.

'He were barely cold in the grave afore we snatched him,' Jack boasted, yanking open the boy's jaw, so he wore a wolfish, skeletal grin. Jack – we called him Crack-Handed Jack on account of his right-hook and his swing with a shovel – waggled the boy's loose tooth and extracted it in one clean, swift motion. He held it under the light of the candle, inspecting it closely.

'A token!' he said, wrapping the bloodied canine in a kerchief and pocketing it inside his long, black coat.

Jack and I had been in the trade for three full winters, when we both stumbled into an opportunity at the Five Bells public house. A stranger tipped us off about a deal with a surgeon at St Bart's Hospital and let us in on how much he earned delivering "packages." Trade had been picking up around the city, but there still weren't enough fresh cadavers to go around.

'I ain't asking no questions,' the corpse-hauler said, blowing his nose loudly and wiping it on a dirty rag.

You never get used to it, the smell. The hot stench of exhumed death. The rancid taste of bile that foams in your throat, causing you to spill your guts in the graveyard. At least I had, the first time.

The boy reeked, of course. The bitter stink of misery, desperation and squalor.

'On the market for ten guineas,' Jack said, closing the boy's jaw like a puppet. 'No use to no-one when he was alive. You'll receive your cut, of course.'

The corpse-hauler ran a tongue across his lip, wiping his glasses with the same 'kerchief. I pressed my fingers over the boy's cold eyelids and withdrew the candle. I always kept the bottle close on nights when I was out on the job and it took a good swig to wash the taste of fetid air out of my mouth.

We had to keep the bodies in the cool and dark, to stop them going bad so quickly. Everyone knew that Old Sam down the Hell's Bells had a hatch out the back, where suspicious packages would some-

times come and go. The yeasty odour from the barrels helped to conceal the funk of rotten meat.

A rat scuttled across the floor, disappearing through a crack in the walls.

'A vagabond?' the corpse-hauler asked, expressing a keen sense of disapproval. 'One less petty thief blighting our streets. I suppose he had no name? No relatives?'

'As easy as falling asleep.' Jack pulled the body bag over the boy's face, so he became just another Thing. An anonymous cadaver to be picked apart over the dissection table, like a carcass being feasted upon by gluttonous vultures.

I took another long slug of rum, trying to picture Mary's face when we boast about our snatch. The way we'd spotted him, sleeping outside down the pig market in Shoreditch. The way he'd followed us blindly, when we promised him lodgings and a hot pork pie. The way he'd sunk softly into my arms, intoxicated by the rag of laudanum.

These hands had robbed the dead plenty of times. But it was the first time I'd ever cheated life from the living.

☠

'Get inside, you quivering fool!' Mary peered at me through the chink with her good eye, before ushering me inside our hovel and bolting the door.

I slunk down at the table, shaking the rain from my jacket like a wet mongrel. ''Ere, get this down ye.' Mary measured out a strong tot of gin and I knocked it back in one gulp. 'Is it done?'

My wife craned over the table, wringing her boney hands. Her good eye was fixed on me, dark and penetrative, while her blind one seemed to gaze out into the darkness and beyond, all-seeing like a mirror. Sometimes, she claimed to have visions: Michael speaking to her from beyond the grave.

The fever had struck them both. Death crept into our home one night, silently, cloaked in black. Plague rattled through the air and the walls. It had fed on my son, greedily and lustily. It left with his life between its pock-ridden hands.

Mary, my wife, was able to fend off the fever, though it had left her partially sighted. A strange occurrence, that meant she would always have one eye on this world and one looking forward to the next.

'It is done.' I spluttered, smacking my fist against my beating chest. *The boy had felt so light in my hands.*

Mary rubbed her hands together, warming herself. 'And no-one saw you with the lad when he was alive?'

'As invisible in a crowd as a ghost.' London was crawling with them, urchins, spending their days trudging through muck like rats or roaches. Sometimes, I envied the dead. 'No-one to come looking for him.'

'Good,' Mary said, her eye seeing right through me. 'Good.'

She took down her physic from the shelf, swilled it back with a wince, before smoothing down her apron. Then, she began to busy around in our humble one-room lodgings, fetching a bowl of water from the dresser.

''Ere, my love.' She began to nurse my hands, rubbing her fingers over their calluses and sores. 'Let's wash these hands of the Devil's work. Rest now, my love. Come to bed.'

I dried my hands on a rag, as she slipped her cold, white paws into mine. This time there was no grave-gravel beneath my nails, only the incurable stain of sin.

☠

That night, I awoke, as if from a fitful, feverish dream. My brow was dripping with perspiration, damp nightclothes clinging to my skin. Mary slept soundly beside me, both eyes closed, her breath sour as turned milk.

Scratch, scratch, creak.

I stumbled out of bed, still woozy from the rum and the gin. I tripped, once, before finding my footing. The candle was beside our bed, but I couldn't remember where we left the matches.

Creak.

The room swooned drunkenly in and out of focus. *A rat?* When I attempted to follow the sounds of the scratching coming from the floorboards, the noise only drifted further away, coming from below. The stairs. *A burglar?*

Now, I may have robbed my fair share of graves, but I'd never filched from the living. *To rob a man while he slept in his own bed...In his coffin...* Meanwhile, my wife dreamed on peacefully unaware, and I felt sure that the effects of her physic meant she would not wake.

Creak. Creak. Creak.

I searched around blindly for something to grab, to strike the intruder with. At once, I came upon my shovel, backed up in the corner, fresh from my nightly haunts in the graveyard. She was stiff and ready in my hands as any weapon, ready to bash out the brains of the offending, villainous scoundrel.

Acting braver than I felt, I hunched behind the door, shovel gripped tightly in my grave-robber's hands.

Thud. Thud. Thud.

Footsteps were pacing up the stairs, getting closer. Perhaps it was just another tenant moving around in the lodgings below? But no. No-one else would think to climb the steps up to the top room, where my wife and I slept, in the dead of the night.

'Who's there?'

The footsteps stopped suddenly. Then, as if on instinct, they drew closer, the creaks growing ever nearer towards our door... Yet, these were not the footsteps of an adult. I could tell, by the soft treading of light feet upon the stairs. The footsteps were softer...and...I could almost swear...

'Michael?' I uttered.

The boy's footsteps paused, right outside our door. I clutched the shovel tighter, as the door handle began to rattle.

'Michael? Michael, have you come home?'

A hand on my shoulder. At once, the rattling stopped, as if the spirit – my child, whatever it was – had drawn back in fear. I exhaled a deep sigh of relief, collapsing upon the weight of my shovel.

My wife. It was only my wife's hand.

'What in the name of our Lord are you doing up?' Her blind eye loomed towards me, luminous as the moon. There was something beautiful and bewitching about her eye. Dull as glass; bluer than day.

'I thought...' I rambled.

'Thought I was sleeping, did ye?' Mary scolded, striking me hard across the cheek. 'Just 'cause I'm blind, don't mean I've lost all me senses! What will folks say, when they 'ear you've been raving like a madman? They'd lock me up afore they did you and don't you know it? Mad-Eyed Mary and her maniac husband! Ha!'

My cheek prickled where she'd struck me; she tended to it with a gentle stroke.

'Our boy...' I muttered, my voice breaking. 'Our boy, our boy. He's so cold...'

'Michael rests peacefully in his grave,' Mary said, her blue eye wide. 'I know, my love. I felt him before. Let him rest.'

She guided me to bed like an invalid, leading the way through the pregnant darkness, her hands tremulous and cold.

🕱

Later that week, I rapped on the door to Jack's apartment. 'Mr Barker?' I called out again. 'Mr Barker, are you there? I wish to attend on a matter of, ahem, *business.*'

The door opened just a crack and the face of Jack's wife, Bess, appeared, looking pale and harassed. Fair curls escaped from under her bonnet, a slash of red across her lips. Her eyes darted around furtively.

'Speak of the Devil,' she hissed. 'What do you want?'

Jack's wife had always disapproved of our business, refusing to acknowledge any morbid matters to do with resurrection or the grave. Hence why my partner and I usually held our meetings on street corners, or in public houses. As long as Jack returned home with money in his pocket, his missus had learnt to ask no questions. Yet I had not received correspondence from my partner in nearly a week, so I was beginning to suspect there was something wrong.

Bessie lowered her voice, pulling the door to and craning her neck towards me. She reeked of musk, like wilting violets. 'Jack's sick, do you 'ear? He's been taken ill. We don't want no folks 'round 'ere.'

'Ill?' I asked, tipping my hat and wiping my brow. 'What ails him?'

'It's all that foul air you keep breathing.' Bess shook her head. 'It's poisoned his lungs. I found blood on his 'kerchief...'

The bloodied rag from where Jack had pulled out the tooth...

'Listen, Mrs B., this is important,' I insisted. 'Could you please report to your husband that...' I looked around once and hushed. 'A young woman in Bethnal Green has just passed on. Pretty thing; a virgin. They bury her in the churchyard of St Stephen's, tomorrow, at noon.'

'My husband is sweating and chattering in his sleep.' Mrs Barker looked about ready to strike me. 'I told 'im, it's a morbid business...'

'Could...?' I pictured the pox that had killed my only child, the corpses of the victims, spotted and scarred. 'Could you tell him...?'

Bessie's eyes flashed. 'I know what you did. And I won't see my husband swing for it neither!'

My vision suddenly began to swim, as the walls shifted in front of me and the ground seemed to wobble. I leant one hand against the wall to right myself, shutting my eyes tight against the pain that split my skull. Within a few moments, Mrs Barker had slammed the door in my face and I had come to, wondering why this sense of fever had suddenly possessed me and if I was really some sort of devil indeed.

I could have done with a gin to steady myself, as I clung to the bannister and hurried downstairs, straight out into the streets for a spell of fresh air. London pulsed and reeked all around me. Coaches careened up and down, as throngs of market-goers teemed into the street, shouting about this and that, calling out their wares. An elderly woman lifted up her skirts to piss by the roadside as a group of ragged boys ran past, jeering. The city festered with crime, poverty and disease.

A young lad slouched in the shadow of a doorway, clad all in rags, his shoes no more than tattered slippers on his feet. He could've been sick, or merely sleeping. He looked no older than Michael – twelve, or thirteen – but already aged by the injustice of the world.

Something about him made me pause in the middle of the street. The bustle of London continued – a couple of lively gents nearly knocking me clean off my feet – but my gaze remained fixed on the boy.

It was as if he were calling out to me, without words. *Michael. My dear boy. Back from the grave.*

Intrepidly, I crossed the street. It was this queer, indiscernible feeling I got that something was calling out to me. Now, I ain't no superstitious fool, though my wife has visions, but I knew this was no mortal encounter. Something from – from the other side – was trying to make its peace with me. I don't know how, I just *knew.*

It was the same spirit who had crept stealthily up my stairs. The same spirit who came like a rogue in the night to disturb my slumber.

The only spirit I have – nor ever will – witness.

When that boy lifted his cap, his face was deathly pale. I could not help but recoil in fear, as a ghastly chill swept over me. For his face was not the face of my loving, unfortunate son, but of the boy *I had killed!* His eyes were wide and empty as the grave. His gaze fixed on mine, as he opened his mouth, lips curling into a vengeful sneer. And – *Oh, what had I done!* – there was a brilliant gap where his stolen tooth should have been!

I knew, then, that the child had come back to haunt me. He had returned to torment me – to plague me – for snatching his life!

I was sure the lad's corpse had been dismembered by now, his limbs festering in some dump of useless anatomical parts. But his *soul* – at least, part of it – was bound to mine eternally. For when you take another life, one becomes dependent upon the other. This spirit would not rest until some sense of balance had been restored.

☠

'What are you doin', creepin' up on me like that?' Mary started before the fire, dropping her needle in her lap.

'What you starin' at, witch?' I snarled, voice laden with drink. 'You barmy old bat!'

''Ere, Robert?' Mary curled into herself. 'What's gotten into you, my love? Come, sit by the fire. You know you ain't right, when you've been on the drink.' Her voice trembled nervously. 'What do you look at me so queer for?'

'It should've killed us both,' I growled, staring into the flickering, ash-hot flames. 'It should've taken me when it took him. How can I spend each day, knowing that my son is dead? I resent the living!'

I leant against the fireplace, curling my hands into fists. This boy – my own mental configuration of guilt – would plague my life until my miserable days were over. What was left to live for?

'Rob?' Mary whimpered. 'You're scaring me.'

She was darning some useless old piece of rag, hunched by the fire, squinting with her one functioning eye. The other roamed around wildly, as if she could not control it. Wretched, pathetic, frightful woman!

'Do you not think I would have died with him?' I turned and glared at my wife. 'Do you not think I would've given my life in exchange for his?'

Mary trembled and reached for her physic, tucked away behind the corner of her chair.

'Drunk old hag!' I kicked it away from her. 'Who are you to curse me for drinking, when you cannot bear the daylight without your poison? O, woman! Must we spend all our lives crouching in the dark?'

She clutched the fabric in her withered hand, crying as the liquid dripped between the cracks in the floorboards.

'Please, love? You would not hurt me?' she begged.

I marched across the room and seized my shovel. I felt the blade between my fingertips, sharp as a knife. 'This is the only tool I need,' I hissed, feeling the weight of the weapon in my hands.

'You would not murder me and dispose of me, as one of your corpses?'

My wife shivered. The shovel was ready and cold, the one tool that separated me from this life and the next.

'We are creatures of the dark, you and I,' I told her. 'We must lurk in shadows, because the sun plagues us and stings your eyes! God forgive me, I have shaken hands with the dark and danced with the Devil. Now my soul will never rest! And if I go to the gibbet tonight, you're sure as hellfire swinging with me.'

Mary cowered and clutched her rat-like claws in front of her face. I took a step towards her – then drew back, watching her whimper before the fire. She yelped, as I tapped my spade once, sharply, against the floorboard.

Then I headed towards the graveyard.

The night was cool and still. A raven perched in the branches of a nearby tree, watching. It cawed once and flapped its wings, before flying off, as if avoiding the sudden waft of incoming death.

I found Michael's grave, small and premature, rising out of the ground like a child's first tooth. There, buried beneath the ground, was my son. His body festering and sinking back into the soil. His flesh becoming food for the worms, while maggots feasted upon his eyes.

I let out a sharp howl, as I dug my shovel into the ground. The moon was high and round. I felt sure that if there were spirits out tonight; they were hungry and active, evaluating my every move.

I pressed my foot upon the blade, and dug.

I dug, and I dug, and I dug. Turfing up soil, the sweat dripping in torrents from my brow, the night air like a cool, relieving breeze against my skin. It was hard work, without the two of us. I had to keep the lantern by my feet and there was nobody there, behind my shoulder, to keep watch. If I went to gaol tonight – I decided – I would not care, if only I had done this one last thing.

Maybe, there would be no eternal rest. For any of us. But that boy had come back from death to tell me one thing. And it was that I must look upon the face of my child one more time.

When they had covered him up in the shroud, I could not bear to look at him. So wasted and deformed was his face, ravaged from the effects of the disease, that he was hardly recognisable. Even the sight of my wife's eye was bad enough. But to see my beautiful son consumed by so much ugliness! Oh, it had plagued my heart!

I wrenched my shovel into the ground and eventually stabbed upon the hard exterior of his humble coffin. My child, my child. Not dead, but merely sleeping.

Rest easy, my boy. Father is here.

As if with the strength of two men, I was able to yank and prize the head of the coffin, until it was possible to slide the lid free.

There, in the ground, lay my son. His body was grey and shrivelled, subject to the grim effects of decay, red hair bristled like straw around his hollow scalp. His lips, black and taut as old leather. His eyelids, frosted shut. His face had become warped on one side, skin rotten with pox, as if the disease had been painted over his body with a cruel brush.

I clasped my arm around my mouth to avoid the stench, even worse than when the living sickness was oozing out of him, in a torrent of puss and shit. My boy, my boy. Here he was, lying dead in his coffin. Where we would all go, one day.

Where, some day, I would surely join him.

In The Bleak Midwinter

by Neil A. Wilson

Lieutenant James Cleithral had a short and bloody war. In 1915 he joined up, and thanks to family connections managed to procure a junior officer's position in the Lancaster Fusiliers – his grandfather's old regiment.

However, by the winter of 1916, after a mustard gas attack, James's war was all but over having been invalided out. He found himself like many others before him convalescing in Marsham Hall.

The hall itself was an extensive sixteenth century manor house with a long-forgotten ancestry, set within a dozen acres or so, some little way outside of Norwich. The single year of war James participated in had irrevocably changed his personality. Gone was the free-spirited youth barely into his twenties, replaced now with the bleak hardness of a war veteran, like many before him, weighed down by the responsibilities of command – a burden to his very soul.

Many a time he would find himself suddenly awake, screaming at the top of his voice, trying to escape from the nightmarish dreams he inhabited – drenched in sweat which penetrated more than the sheets upon which he lay. His mind constantly focussed on the terrors of exploding bodies ripped apart by enemy shell fire. Those left in no-man's-land torn and shredded, covered with flies and the ever-crawling host of maggots. Always his mind was filled with the stench of decay, yet ever alert for the tell-tale trace of mustard gas. But he was lucky, or so the nurses frequently reminded him, for he was alive and back home – safe.

He wheezed like an old man with every shuffling step he took, though his youthful strength was returning to him – slowly. During the day, we would often play cards with his fellow inmates, or take a short walk around the grounds. A nurse ever attentive and pushing a wheelchair would follow him, in case of any sudden relapse.

But it was at night that the terrors he had witnessed would yet again take a tortuous hold over him. The moans and groans combined with the sudden shouts of distressed patients reverberated around the darkened dormitory wards, a constant reminder of the hell he was trying to leave behind. These continuous nightly interruptions allowed for little sleep or respite from the horrors of his memories. Often, he would secretly get up and walk about the hallways and corridors, skilfully dodging the night nurses and doctors.

It was on one of these occasions that I first encountered him. I found James wandering the corridors on the upper disused floors in search of a little peace and quiet. Over several weeks of wandering his ambivalence towards me changed and what started as a brief nod towards a fellow nocturnal sufferer developed into polite conversation, which culminated with him telling me his entire life story.

He spoke in an embittered voice at some length of all his hopes and dreams for a hap-py life, now smashed because of the mustard gas in the war to end all wars. But it quickly became apparent to me that James was holding something back. Indeed, with every meeting, he seemed if anything to be more troubled in his mind. A feeling that only grew stronger with each occasion we met.

Secretly over the weeks he continued to visit me night after night. With every passing day that I saw him his body grew physically stronger, but his mind – the very essence of his will – seemed to diminish slightly. Then one night he told me of his recurring dream, or should I say, nightmare? In all my years, I have never come across such horrific pain and anguish. It drew me closer to him, for such a tormented soul in one so young was way beyond my wildest imaginings.

I endeavoured to do all that I could for James, even visiting him during the day. His fitful slumber so full of dreams became lucid and almost real to him, so much so that they began to disturb the other patients. Eventually the doctors were left with no other recourse but to move him into a side room, where he was placed under constant super-vision.

I visited him day after day, as I appeared to be his only friend. I talked to him in my most calming voice, whispering in his ear as I stroked his forehead. Each day I tried to convince him that his nightmares, now daymares, were just dreams and nothing to worry about. But his delusions only grew with every day of constant attention that I gave him. Eventually, even in his most lucid of moments, he could not tell the difference between what was real and what was a tor-tured fantasy.

Often, he would push me away with immense strength, as only a deranged and deluded soul could do. But I was determined as his friend to see his torment through to some sort of final resolution – no matter what.

Shortly after this he began to wildly flail his arms about, as if fighting some unseen spectral antagonist. The doctors and nurses, fearful of self-harm, tied his arms down to the bed. His frustration in not being able to move his limbs only agitated his restless mind further – but still I did all that I could for him.

The delusions increased as his mind became ever weaker. During his failing lucid moments, he would fitfully shout out in a gasping voice: "The hood is mine, the hood is mine!"

Realising he meant his gas mask hood, I tried to encourage him to let it go, whispering in his ear constantly: "No. The hood is mine, not yours." But my attempts to calm him only seemed to agitate his fevered mind to greater heights of anxiety.

The doctors were concerned that in his delirious state, James was not getting enough sleep, eventually deciding to drug him into a morphine oblivion. To me this approach seemed further detrimental to his health, allowing as it did for his own personal nightmare to get a firmer grip on his psyche. I could feel the line between the realms of reality and nightmares slowly dwindling into some amorphous, tumultuous mass with each twist and turn of his fevered brow.

The next day I felt a change within him, and I knew my constant battle with the hood was finally going my way. I fancied I caught glimpses of him fighting with another man, as the yellow fog spilled over the edge of the cratered hole. The reeking deadly grip of the mustard gas as it slowly advanced, staining the pockets of un-melted snow an ever-deepening shade of yellow. Its clawing tentacles twisting in the currents of air, seeking out any form of breathing life. All this in direct contrast to the rapid, continuous battle to force the hood over his own head against the dwindling ferocity of his unknown foe.

Day after day this relentless ghoulish struggle continued. I could feel James's fitful screams within his drugged mind as the thick gas obscured all but his opponent's outstretched clawing hand – which came protruding out of the dense yellowing miasma.

Seeing through his eyes he looked out aghast via the two round, plate glass eye coverings of the protective hood. The single hand reached out further from the deepening yellow fog, its middle fingernail tapping on the glass lens in a frantic plea to be let in.

Then the hand was gone, falling away to where the gas was densest. But no matter how hard James's rasping breath wheezed from beneath the hood, the faint noise of the fingernails' infernal tapping upon the glass could still be heard deep within the recesses of his own mind.

"Doctor, it appears he has finally gone," a nurse said, feeling for a pulse. The doctor in the doorway came forward and listened to James's chest.

"Yes, nurse," he concurred. "A blessed relief in this case. He showed so much promise of a full recovery early on, I really thought we stood a good chance with this one." The doctor took the stethoscope from his ears and hung it about his neck. "You know, I think the problem started when he began flailing his arms about."

"Yes, doctor, it always seems to take them that way... Such a pity, like all the others, so young and full of life."

I left them there over the body of my friend and resumed my nightly patrol. As I looked out of the upper corridor windows, it began snowing again. I wondered how many times it had snowed since I became a resident here, all those centuries ago. Was I truly just a nightmare for all those who encountered me?

CONTRIBUTORS

★ ★ ★

ANDREW ROBINSON is a printmaker and graphic designer. A self-taught artist specialising in linocut prints, his interests and influences stem from wildlife, mythology, and all things creepy or otherworldly. Andrew hails from the east coast of Canada and now lives in Oxford, England, with his partner and daughters. A selection of his work can be seen at *monografik.ca* and on Instagram *@eaglesnakefight*.

REBECCA PARFITT has worked in publishing for over a decade. By day, she is Commissioning Editor for Honno - the UK's longest running women's press; by night she haunts the desk at Ghastling Towers. She is a writer, editor and director, currently working on a horror screenplay and a book of macabre short stories for which she won a Writers' Bursary from Literature Wales in 2020. Two stories from this collection were published in *The New Gothic Review* in 2020. Her first film, *Feeding Grief to Animals*, was produced in 2021 by the BBC & FfilmCymruWales - of which she was writer and director. She lives in the Llynfi Valley, South Wales, with her partner and two young children. *Rebeccaparfitt.com*

WALLACE MCBRIDE is a graphic designer from South Carolina, USA. His work has been featured in *Fangoria*, The Sleepy Hollow International Film Festival, The Boston Comedy Festival, the Associated Press, the U.S. Army and dozens of newspapers in the United States, and also used on licensed merchandise for *The Prisoner* and *Star Trek*. He is the creator of The Collinsport Historical Society, a website dedicated to the cult television series *Dark Shadows*. Since its launch in 2012, The Collinsport Historical Society has been recognised numerous times by The Rondo Hatton Classic Horror Awards, and received The Silver Bolo Award in 2020 from Shudder's *The Last Drive-In with Joe Bob Briggs*. Wallace sometimes uses the handle 'Unlovely Frankenstein', which is either a pseudonym or just the name of his Etsy store. He isn't sure yet. *www.wallacemcbride.com*

TRACEY REES is an aspiring writer of short stories and poetry and works as an editor for an online medical education provider. Tracey joined The Ghastling team as an editorial assistant in 2022. She lives with her husband and two feline friends near the whispering woods in South Wales, where she can often be found seeking out nocturnal animals for morbid conversations during her bouts of insomnia. When not busy doing those things Tracey is passionate about classic horror movies, spooky tales, travelling, drinking tea, and rearranging the furniture.

MARK BLAYNEY won the Somerset Maugham Award for *Two Kinds of Silence*. Recent fiction and poetry collections are *Doppelgangers* and *Loud music makes you drive faster* with Parthian, and *The view from my shed* with Dreich Chapbooks. He was a Hay Festival Writer at Work, has won a Wales Media Award for his journalism and now works as a Royal Literary Fund Fellow, tutoring writing skills. *@markblayney* *www.markblayney.weebly.com*

JP RELPH is a working-class Cumbrian writer mostly hindered by four cats and aided by copious tea. She volunteers in a charity shop where they let her dress mannequins and have first dibs on haunted objects. A forensic science degree and passion for microbes, insects and botany often influence her words. Recently found in *New Flash Fiction Review, Noctivagant Press* and *Molotov Cocktail*. @RelphJp

VICTORIA DOWD is the award-winning author of the bestselling Smart Woman's Mystery series. Her debut novel, *The Smart Woman's Guide to Murder*, won The People's Book Prize for fiction 2021 and was named In Search of the Classic Mystery Novel's Book of the Year 2020. Victoria was awarded the Gothic Fiction prize for her short fiction and her work has been published in many literary journals. She is also the author of the Adapting Agatha series which has seen her speak at many literary festivals, including The International Agatha Christie Festival and this year's Crimefest.

REGGIE CHAMBERLAIN-KING is a writer, musician, and archivist of the unusual, publishing three books with Blackstaff Press: *Weird Belfast* (2014) and *Weird Dublin* (2015), and the collection *The Black Dreams: Strange Stories from Northern Ireland* (2021). With composer Martin White, Reggie brought E.T.A. Hoffman's fever dream, *Master Flea*, to the London stage as a musical and an adaptation of J.S. Le Fanu's *Green Tea* was released through Swan River Press in 2019. Reggie is a regular contributor to BBC Radio Ulster and presents documentaries on the strange for BBC Radio 4.

WARREN BENEDETTO writes dark fiction about horrible people, horrible places, and horrible things. He is an award-winning author and a full member of the SFWA. His stories have appeared in publications such as *Dark Matter Magazine, The Dread Machine,* and *Haven Spec*; on podcasts such as *The NoSleep Podcast, Tales to Terrify,* and *The Creepy Podcast*; and in anthologies from *Apex Magazine, Scare Street, Eerie River Publishing,* and more. His hobbies include sleeping, hitting snooze, sleeping some more, and naps. For more information, visit *www.warrenbenedetto.com* and follow @warrenbenedetto on Twitter and Instagram.

EVE CHANCELLOR is an English Teacher in Manchester. She has a First in English from the University of Liverpool and an MLitt in Victorian Literature from the University of Glasgow. Her short stories are published on *East of the Web* and *Reflex Press*. Her poetry is featured in multiple publications, including: *Apricot Press, Dream Catcher, Hyacinth Review* and *Ink, Sweat and Tears*.

RORY SAY is a Canadian writer of short fiction whose work tends toward the dark, strange, and speculative. Stories of his have recently appeared in *On Spec, Uncharted, Lucent Dreaming,* and *Short Fiction*: The Visual Literary Journal, as well as on podcasts such as *NoSleep* and *Nocturnal Transmissions*. A short chapbook collection, titled "The Marksman", is forthcoming from *Red Bird Chapbooks*. Read more by visiting his website: *rorysay.com*

NEIL A. WILSON has always written short stories and poems for pleasure. In 2018, 'Diary of a Dead Man' was included in The Ghastling Book VIII anthology. Currently, he is writing the third in a series of four fantasy novels, *The Towers of the Four Winds*. He has published two books of poetry: *Pithy and Other Paraphernalia: Part One* (2017) and *Paraphernalia: Another Fifty Poems: Part Two* (2017) via Amazon CreateSpace. In addition, 'A Flower in the Field of War' was published as a flash fiction story by Forward Poetry in *Flash Fiction* (2015). Prior to this, Forward Poetry published 'Home of Aspirations' in *The Great British Write Off, Home is Where the Heart is* anthology (2014); and 'An Ode to the Spider and its Web' in *An Ode To Anthology* (2014).

PAUL BUCHANAN'S short fiction has appeared in *Storyquarterly, Marlboro Review, Portland Review, Cicada,* and many other literary journals. My nonfiction has appeared in such magazines as *Writers Digest, Los Angeles Magazine, History Magazine* and *Orange Coast*. His recent novel, *City of Fallen Angels*, received a starred review in *Publishers Weekly*.

It's Amazing!

The low cost of supporting

The Ghastling!

For just pennies a day you can support
the morbid interests of horror fans all over the world

VISIT WWW.PATREON.COM/THEGHASTLING
TO FIND OUT HOW YOU CAN BECOME A GHASTLING

LAST NAME OF AUTHOR
Issue 17
The Ghastling
BOOK TITLE
STAMP LIBRARY OWNERSHIP